Fraud

and

Feta

Michelle Ford

FRAUD AND FETA

Kinglet Books
Victoria BC, Canada
Copyright © 2023 Michelle Ford
Cover design by GetCovers

ISBN: 978-1989677438 (print paperback)
ISBN: 978-1989677773 (ebook)
ISBN: 978-1989677797 (large print paperback)
ISBN: 978-1989677780 (print hardcover)

First edition: August 2023

Chapter 1

Brianna West pulled her sweater's zipper higher against the chill of the late autumn air. Winter was coming to Driftwood Island and coming fast. That her ferry trip from the mainland had clear skies was nothing short of a miracle.

"Thanks for coming along with me to Vancouver," her friend Macy Jones said. She tucked her gloved hands under her arms and raised her face to the sun. "Quick, soak up the rays before the sun drops below the horizon."

Brianna raised her face to the glow of the afternoon sun, low on the horizon this late in November. Her brown curls jostled around her face, and she brushed them back absently. Seagulls cried, and the scent of saltwater filled the air. Only a few hardy souls joined them on the outer deck in the bracing sea breeze. The rest of the passengers huddled inside, waiting for the ferry to dock at Driftwood Island.

"I'm glad we went," Brianna said to Macy. "I desperately needed some new clothes."

"The selection is way better in the city than in Snuggler's Cove." Macy chuckled and pushed her blonde hair out of her eyes. "Belinda's Boutique can have some fun stuff occasionally. But sometimes her eye for fashion is—how should I say it—an acquired taste."

"I'm not always in the mood for neon florals,"

Brianna agreed.

A man wearing tan trousers and a fluorescent safety vest walked by. He stopped when he saw them. "Macy Jones," he said, his salt and pepper moustache waggling. "It's been an age. How are you?"

"Rolling right along," she replied. "It's good to see you, Ben. Meet my friend Brianna. She opened the Golden Moon café in the summer."

"I haven't tried it yet," Ben said.

"Well, you're missing out." Macy shook her head with a regretful air. "Best baked goods on the island, and I'm including Hilltop Farm's cinnamon buns."

Brianna appreciated her friend's staunch support at all turns. "I'm still ironing out the details, but it's going well."

"I'll check it out some time," Ben promised. "I'm based in Vancouver now, not on Driftwood, but I still visit occasionally."

A couple walked by. The man's booming voice didn't leave any room for Brianna's reply, and the woman's cackling laughter drowned out thought. Once they'd passed, Macy caught Brianna's eye and snickered.

"Not a pair of delicate flowers," she said.

"They were nothing," Ben said with a shake of his head. "You should have heard the two who came on the ferry yesterday. So loud and obnoxious. Pushing past customers, yelling at each other across the deck, cutting lines like they owned the place. They even had a shouting match between them—some disagreement over who knows what. It was 'John' this, and 'idiot' that. Horrible people."

"What a nightmare," said Macy. "I guess that's customer service for you. Oh, no, what if they come into the café?"

"As long as they buy plenty of food, I can put up with noise," Brianna said.

Macy continued to chat with Ben while the ferry drew closer to Driftwood Island. Brianna's stomach rumbled, and she remembered with a start the spanakopita she'd tucked in her bag from a bakery in Vancouver. She'd recently started making the flaky feta and spinach-filled pastries at the Golden Moon, and she wanted to see how hers stacked up. She hadn't been hungry then, but she liked to plan ahead. Besides which, the bakery had smelled too good to resist.

It was market research, she argued to herself as she unwrapped the spanakopita from its paper bag. She needed to keep abreast of the latest pastry developments in her industry.

Crispy cheese decorated the edge of the golden phyllo pastry, and hints of green filling lined the fold. As a connoisseur of fine pastries, Brianna nodded approvingly at the perfectly crafted triangle. She took a deep sniff, savoring the full-bodied scent of feta and spinach. Then she bit into the golden crust.

Three chews later, she nearly gasped aloud. This was perfection. This was heaven. She hadn't known how good spanakopita could taste until this moment. Buttery flakiness melted into a pungent, savory cheese flavor heightened by the earthiness of spinach. Her first reaction was of pure bliss.

Her second reaction dampened her joy. How had the

bakers of this marvel crafted such a fine specimen? More importantly, why wasn't Brianna's own spanakopita this good?

Something shriveled inside her. What was she doing, pretending to bake? If she couldn't produce masterpieces like this pastry, did she deserve to host a café like the Golden Moon? Was she a fraud?

A seagull watched her with beady eyes, waiting for her to drop a flake of pastry. Part of her wanted to toss her treat to the bird in a fit of pique. She jammed the rest into her mouth instead and glared at the seagull. No way was she going to waste this pinnacle of cheesy glory on a bird.

The seagull flapped away in disgust. Brianna was left to chew her food and ruminate on her failings as a successful baker.

A few days later, Brianna surveyed the bustling outdoor market with a contented smile, her spanakopita worries momentarily buried. Despite the cold, plenty of island residents wandered the market stalls on soggy grass outside the community hall of Snuggler's Cove. Most of the local artisans were present, showcasing a variety of pottery, knitted items, late season produce, and baking. Brianna had thought about running a stall here for her café's goods, but she hadn't had the time this season. If things were good next year, she'd consider it.

A fishmonger opened her cooler at the next stall, and Brianna walked over to look. She shifted the wicker basket on her arm, feeling both terribly twee and right at home with the basket. Her acquaintances in Vancouver would laugh at her, but she was far from the only one with a basket at this market. She would rather fit in on Driftwood Island than avoid scorn in the big city. This was now her home, and every day brought a new reason to love it here.

"Do you have any scraps?" Brianna asked the fishmonger after she finished with her customer and turned, smiling, to greet Brianna. "I wanted a treat for my cat." Her ginger cat, Paprika, would adore a morsel of fresh fish.

"I have a few heads in the back cooler for fish bait," the woman said, turning to rummage in the cooler behind her. "Let me see."

"And a fillet of lingcod, if you have it," Brianna added. "For me, not the cat."

"I'll see if I can do better than heads for you." The woman winked at her and pulled out a slab of fish. "Will that do?"

"Perfect." Brianna paid for her purchases and tucked them into her basket, resisting the urge to whistle cheerily. That was one step too far. She might as well skip while she was at it. The basket was enough island charm for now.

She wandered through the stalls, greeting acquaintances from the café and town as she meandered. Hilda Button, the elderly proprietor of the Bumblebee Bed and Breakfast and a fellow member of the Gourmand Society—a glorified cheese club Brianna was part of—hobbled past with her own basket.

"Brianna, my dear," she cried. Her glad smile creased her finely lined face into a map of wrinkles. She patted her tightly curled white hair. "When are you going to open a stall here? The only other foods today are Beth's granola and those strange frozen mangos on a stick. It's far too cold for that nonsense, although the children seem to like it."

She pointed at a pair of young ones who darted past, their mouths sticky and yellow and their hands clutching half-chewed mangos on skewers.

Brianna shook her head. "One day, when I get my act together. Oaklyn is running the café this morning, though, so you're welcome to pop by after this."

"I might. I very well might." Hilda pointed behind her along Brianna's path. "Don't forget to visit Costas Dimitriou's stall today. His kiwis are finally ripe, and they look divine." She rummaged in her basket and extracted a hairy, brown fruit. "Well, they don't look like much here, but Costas has a few sliced open for show. Such a splendid green. He's been building that kiwi farm for the past few years—a very diligent young man—and his crop is finally producing. He's a quiet one, not one for talk, but pleasant enough. Go on, make sure you buy a few."

Brianna assured her she would and continued on her way. She chuckled to herself about Hilda's disapproval of quiet people who kept to themselves. Hilda was the town gossip and kept herself abreast of everyone's news. Not knowing Costas's history must have been torturous to her.

Costas's stall was hard to miss. A vibrant green banner draped from the tent's top with the words "Kiwi Ridge

Orchard" in brilliant white. Large baskets of kiwis filled the creaking table. As Hilda had mentioned, a plate with sliced kiwis attractively arranged in a circle graced center stage. A man with a dark beard and wavy hair stood behind the table. A purple birthmark peeked out from his beard onto his cheekbone. His bright eyes and cheerful smile invited her closer.

"Good morning," Brianna said to him. "I hear you have local kiwis for sale."

"Of course," he said in a slight accent. "Most of what I grow are fuzzy kiwis. Sweet and flavorful. Great in fruit salad, in a smoothie, or just on their own eaten with a spoon. I also have a few arguta kiwis, which are small, eaten like grapes."

"They look delicious." Brianna gingerly picked up a fruit and sniffed it. "How come I haven't seen you at the market before? I wouldn't have missed your stall."

"Kiwis aren't harvested until the first frost of autumn," he said in a mournful tone. "Then they take a while to ripen off the vine. And this is the last market of the season, too. It's a hurdle I'll have to figure out if I want to sell them on Driftwood Island. I'm in talks with the Apple Cart grocery store, so hopefully they will stock my produce for the next few months as the fruits ripen."

"That is unfortunate," Brianna agreed. "What made you decide to grow kiwis? It's an unusual fruit."

"But perfect for this climate." Costas grew animated at Brianna's attention on what was clearly a favorite topic of his. "Kiwis are grown commercially in New Zealand, which has a very similar climate to southern British Columbia. The right amount of rain and temperature.

There are a few local growers on the bigger Victoria Island, but none near Driftwood. And kiwis are quite popular."

"These are gorgeous photos of the fruit." Brianna pointed at enlargements of close-ups showcasing the brilliant green fruits and their black seeds.

Costas smiled beatifically. "I love photography. Normally, I take pictures of birds—so many wonderful ones come through here on their yearly migrations—but still-life photos are much easier!"

Another customer approached, and Brianna allowed Costas to handle the transaction while she carefully chose the largest and ripest fruits. Her mouth watered at the thought of enjoying these for breakfast the next day. Or maybe dessert tonight if she couldn't wait that long. Lunch was also a distinct possibility.

"I'll take these," she said when Costas was available again. She handed him the four fruits. "How long did it take before the kiwi vines started producing enough fruit to sell?"

"Four years," he said cheerfully. "I planted them as soon as I moved here from Greece. It was a long-term investment, that's for sure. But it's paying off now. If I get that deal with the Apple Cart."

"Greece, hey? I haven't been, but it looks so beautiful."

His face darkened. "Greece is beautiful, but it was not a good situation at home," he said after a pause. "I needed space from my family."

"That's a big space," Brianna said. She searched for something to say to steer the conversation back to topics that didn't distress the kiwi farmer. "And now you're on Driftwood Island."

Costas beamed. "It is lovely here. Peaceful, and most people are very friendly. Growing up, I spent my summers in the countryside, and it is where I feel most at home."

A booming voice echoed through the stalls.

"I'll be done when I'm done, Gloria. Don't nag me."

A shrill voice answered, but the general bustle of the market drowned it out. Brianna opened her mouth to continue her conversation with Costas, whom she was enjoying speaking with, but the booming voice materialized into a tall, lean man in his thirties. His face was gaunt and his eyes sharp under a thin spread of sandy-colored hair.

The man's eyes focused on Costas and narrowed with avaricious interest. Without consideration for the people he pushed into, he barged through the crowd and headed straight for the green kiwi stall.

"Kiwi farmer," he said abruptly. "What's your name?"

Costas shared a bewildered glance with Brianna before answering. "Costas. Can I help you?"

"I'm John. That's a Greek accent you have, isn't it?" John said. "Where in Greece are you from?"

Brianna stared at the newcomer. Was he born in a barn? His manners were atrocious and clearly made Costas uncomfortable.

"I'm sorry," she said with heat. "But I wasn't finished with my conversation with Costas. You'll have to wait your turn."

"I'll just be a minute." John waved without looking at

Brianna. "I've traveled around Greece a fair bit myself. So, where is it? Macedonia? The Athens area? Thebes, maybe?"

Costas paled, and Brianna took charge.

"I don't see that where Costas is from is any of your business," she said firmly. "I must insist you stop pestering this stall keeper, or I will have to call the police on charges of harassment. Now, are you going to buy some kiwis or not?"

John finally looked at her. He ran his eyes up and down her body. It wasn't in a predatory way but more of a threat assessment, to see if she was a worthy adversary. He must have considered her so because he stepped back.

"Fine," he said with a sniff. He turned and shouted at a bleach-blonde woman wearing cherry red lipstick who peered with an upturned nose at a nearby stall filled with handcrafted jewelry. "Come on, Gloria, we're done here."

"Well, I'm not," she said peevishly. "But I'm certainly done at this stall. What a load of tat."

She stalked after her companion, and the jewelry maker stared with indignation. Brianna caught her eye and shrugged with a sympathetic glance. Were these the people Ben had mentioned on the ferry? She couldn't believe there were two such obnoxious couples roaming around Driftwood Island.

"I'm sorry you had to deal with that," Brianna said to Costas.

"Thank you for helping," he said with a grateful smile. "He was very unpleasant. Enjoy your kiwis."

Chapter 2

The next day, Brianna pulled her coat closer around her while she walked back from the bank to the Golden Moon. The wind whipped across the wide bay of Snuggler's Cove. This time of year, no brightly colored umbrellas dotted the promenade, and nobody sold ice cream. The wind stormed and rain threatened.

Brianna took a deep, bracing breath of salty air. Others might huddle inside at this stormy time of year, but she relished the wildness and chilly breezes that blew away the cobwebs of an indolent summer. She loved the fresh excitement of wind and the promise of warming up in front of fires—electric though hers might be in the café—and sipping hot chocolate. Curling up with her cat Paprika and a book while a storm raged outside her float home sounded heavenly.

"Brianna!" Her aunt's familiar voice stopped Brianna in her tracks. She turned and smiled broadly at Dot Dubois. Her grin only stretched wider at Dot's companion. Zola the goat, a collar around her white neck attached to a leash, trotted at her aunt's side. The miniature animal barely came up to Dot's knee.

"Brisk day for a walk, isn't it?" Dot panted once she'd caught up. Her short, blonde hair streaked with white danced in the wind, and her thick woolen poncho was a beacon of colorful cheer in the dim light of the overcast day. "But Zola doesn't mind. We needed to get off the farm for a bit. Errands to run and all that. I thought about getting my hair cut, but I don't trust that Zola would stay put outside. She's such a little Houdini."

"Can't argue with that." Brianna bent to scratch the goat on her forehead. Zola butted her hand for more when she stopped, and Brianna obliged. "I'm on my way back to the café. Want to stop in to warm up?"

"I will take you up on that later. We're headed to the liquor store first, then the bank." Dot smiled at her. "But then, yes. Can I install a proper hook in your alley to tie up Zola? I feel like that drainpipe isn't enough to keep her secure."

Brianna shuddered at the memory of Zola calmly eating cheese and crackers on her café's kitchen counter when she'd escaped her bonds. "That's a great idea. Grab something suitable the next time you're at the hardware store, and I'll install it."

Brianna pushed Zola's questing teeth away from her jeans and stood upright. A stranger glanced with surprise at the goat on a leash, but the townsfolk she recognized waved at Dot without a second look at Zola. It wasn't the first time Dot had brought the tiny goat to town, not by a long shot.

A familiar figure walked purposefully across the street two blocks away. Corporal Devon Moore's crisp uniform and straight bearing were eye-catching, and his cap half-obscured his glossy dark hair. She and Devon had worked together on solving crimes in the past, and he was a welcome sight around town. Brianna thought about raising her hand to wave, but he hadn't noticed her yet and was too far away to hear her call.

"Who's that?" Dot peered after Brianna's gaze, then chuckled. "It's that handsome Mountie, is it?"

"Is he? I hadn't noticed," Brianna lied. Devon might be easy on the eyes, but he was currently dating Cecelia Yang from the post office and not available. Also, Brianna had no interest in dating anyone at this stage. She was still smarting from her last love interest and had vowed to give herself some time.

"That's quite the reaction." Dot squinted at Devon, who had stiffened and stopped in the middle of the sidewalk. "What did he see?"

Another figure approached him. Brianna narrowed her eyes as she recognized John from the market. Did Devon know the obnoxious man? If he did, they certainly weren't friends because neither man offered handshakes or an embrace. The two men spoke to each other, and Brianna ached to hear the words.

Finally, John's booming shout of angry words echoed down the street. Devon stalked off with John staring after him, his expression twisted into a sneer.

"That was a happy reunion," Dot murmured to Brianna. "I wonder what the history of that relationship is? No, Zola, not my new poncho."

"I wonder," Brianna said. Devon and John clearly knew each other, but not in a friendly way. Brianna had no reason to pry, but she was tempted. If only she and Devon were on closer terms, she could solve this little mystery.

Brianna shook her head and said goodbye to her aunt. She and Devon weren't that close, and that was fine. She wasn't looking for anything more than the friendly acquaintance they already had.

Flour drifted in the air as Brianna unrolled phyllo sheets onto her floured butcher block. Her forehead creased in concentration. The muffins and baked goods for the day were in her temperamental industrial oven or cooling on racks, but this project was her new obsession. Ever since tasting that spanakopita from the Vancouver bakery that had taken her breath away, she'd been determined to create a similar pastry: delightfully savory, incredibly buttery, and all-round crispy perfection. She could hardly show her face in the Golden Moon serving the spanakopita she did. She hadn't wanted to bake her usual ones early that morning, but she needed something to sell today.

If she didn't figure this out, though, she wouldn't have customers for long. The Golden Moon was new enough to still be a novelty. Once that wore off, the townsfolk might desert her for tastier venues. She couldn't rest on her laurels.

Brianna brushed melted butter over the first sheet of phyllo then layered another sheet on top. To achieve spanakopita perfection, she needed to figure out this recipe. It had crossed her mind to call the city bakery and ask for tips. But why would they tell her and risk losing their competitive edge? No, she needed to solve this on her own.

Her employee Teri had arrived and was preparing for the day ahead in the dining area when Brianna slid her tray of spanakopita triangles into the oven and set her timer. Her phone rang, and she answered it.

"Hi, Macy. Aren't you on your way to work by now?"

"I am," she said in a hushed voice. "I mean, I was. Then I found"—she gulped—"a body in the ditch."

Chapter 3

Macy's voice through the phone rose with barely suppressed hysteria. "What do I do? It's a dead body. In the ditch. I called the police, but do I stay near the body or back off? Do I have to keep the birds away from it?"

Despite the lurch in her gut at Macy's words, Brianna kept her voice calm and level. "Where are you?"

"Along the stretch before the Apple Cart. I had to pick up some fruit for the kids today before work." Macy breathed heavily.

"Stay right there. Call your work once you hang up with me. I'll come as soon as I can."

Macy gabbled her thanks and hung up. Brianna yanked off her apron, grabbed her timer, and raced to the dining room.

"Teri," she gasped. "Can you take the spanakopita out when the timer goes off? Everything else is ready in the kitchen. I have to go. Macy needs my help with something."

"Of course," Teri said at once, her cheerful face set in a determined expression. "Go, do what you need to do. I know what I'm doing here."

Brianna thrust the timer at her and ran to fetch her coat and purse. A minute later, she was pedaling as hard as she could through town toward the Apple Cart.

Macy had parked on a quiet back lane leading to the main road. Gentle fields of hay and rows of fruit trees, interspersed with stands of conifers, dark and tall in the autumn grayness, surrounded it. A red barn was a splash of color on this otherwise grim day.

Macy's small red hatchback squatted on the grassy shoulder next to an overgrown ditch half-filled with sluggishly flowing water. The heavy scent of mud and damp permeated the air. Wire fencing delineated public land from the adjacent farm. Rain threatened but held off for now, for which Brianna was thankful. She hadn't put on rain pants for her ride, and her purse sat exposed in the basket behind her.

Brianna pulled her bicycle in front of the car and flicked the kickstand. Macy unfolded from the driver's seat, looking pale and shaken.

"The body is over there." She pointed to the other side of the car. "In the ditch. It's horrible."

"Stay here. I want to take a quick look," Brianna said.

"No, I'm fine." Macy swallowed and straightened her shoulders. "I've already seen it, so it's not like I'll see some fresh horror."

Brianna threw her a questioning look, but Macy nodded resolutely. Without further words, Brianna walked slowly around the car. Her gaze scanned the ditch. When it landed on a head of wet, sandy-colored hair, her heart thundered in her chest. Bile rose in her throat as her view of the body increased.

"It's John," she breathed. "That visitor I saw in the market. You know, the loud one Ben was telling us about on the ferry."

John's hair and clothes were sodden, as if he'd been out all night. His skin was a waxy white. His legs were in the running water of the ditch, but he hadn't stumbled in and died. Nor had a killer tossed him.

Instead, his arms were neatly folded over his chest. His torso rested on the ditch's slope. A vine of some sort encircled his bruised throat. Something white covered his eyes. Brianna peered closer. Were those slices of feta cheese?

Sirens wailed in the distance. Brianna stepped back, nauseated at the sight.

"You called the cops, I hear," she said to Macy. "Good."

"Why would somebody do something like that?" Macy's voice wavered.

Brianna wrapped an arm around her shoulder and steered her until the car was between them and the body. "It's pretty sick," she agreed. "How did you see him from the road?"

"A raven was swooping down, maybe to examine the body. I love birds, so I pulled over to have a look. Then I spotted his red jacket." Macy shuddered and tucked her hands under her arms.

The sirens drew closer. When a police cruiser crested the nearest hill, Brianna waved at it. The vehicle slowed and parked on the shoulder behind Macy.

Devon and another Mountie Brianna recognized as Constable Lenox exited the car and walked over to Brianna and Macy.

"You called emergency services?" Devon asked. His eyes scoured them and the surrounds, his forehead creased. "Something about a body. Are you two all right?"

"We're fine," Brianna assured him. "The body is in the ditch. He's definitely dead and has been for some time."

Devon led the way around Macy's hatchback with Lenox on his heels. When Devon froze, Lenox bumped into him.

"What are you doing?" Lenox grumbled. "This isn't your first dead body."

"It's John Albright," Devon breathed.

Brianna edged closer to the two Mounties to hear their conversation and see Devon's expression better. His wide eyes blinked rapidly, and his jaw hung with astonishment.

Lenox peered at the body. "What, did you know the guy? How well?"

"Well enough." Devon shook his head like something was on it. "Not lately, but I knew him years ago."

Lenox sighed and pulled out his cell phone. "I'll call for backup and secure the scene. You go ask the women what they saw."

Devon nodded, still staring at John's corpse. He finally tore his gaze away and turned his back on the unpleasant sight.

"Are you okay?" Brianna asked. Her mouth twisted in sympathy. She didn't know what was going on, but his distress was palpable.

"I'm fine." Devon heaved a breath, then his gaze sharpened, and he pulled a notebook from his vest pocket. "Ms. Jones, can you describe for me how you discovered the body?"

While Macy launched into her story and Devon asked

her probing questions, Brianna watched Lenox drive short stakes into the ground and drape warning tape between them. Her gaze drifted to John's inert body. Now that the initial shock was over, she could stare at it without her gut roiling. It was no worse than television if she didn't think too hard about it.

The slices of crumbling white cheese covering each eye perplexed her, as did John's formal positioning, as if he were a pharaoh in a sarcophagus. What had the murderer been thinking? It looked eerily composed. Brianna swallowed back nausea.

And what had John been strangled with, if indeed that was his mode of death? Brianna squinted at the vine around his neck, not daring to get closer with Lenox watching the scene. Devon's voice brought her attention back to him.

"What did you see, Brianna?" he asked. "When did you arrive?"

"Macy called me about fifteen minutes ago. I rode my bike here as fast as I could. I didn't touch anything, and we waited for you to arrive."

"Do you need anything else from me?" Macy said. Her face was pale, and she avoided looking at the body in the ditch. "It's just that I'm terribly late for work."

"That's everything," Devon assured her. "Please call if you think of anything else, and we may be in touch with further questions."

Macy hugged Brianna, then hopped in her car and drove off. Brianna looked at Devon with a tilted head. "How did you know this guy?" she asked.

"I knew John years ago," Devon said. He tucked his

notebook in his vest without meeting her eyes. "Back east. I haven't seen him for a decade, at least."

"What do you think happened here?" It hadn't escaped Brianna that Devon hadn't properly answered her question, but she changed the topic to ease his clearly troubled mind. Maybe she could weasel the truth out of him later, when John's body wasn't lying in a ditch beside them.

"I can't speculate," Devon said automatically. His mouth twitched at Brianna's exasperated look. "You know I can't. But let the detectives handle this one, all right?"

"That's what they get paid for," Brianna agreed. "I bake pastries for a living."

She had no desire to solve the mystery of John's demise. Okay, that was a lie—his mysterious circumstances fanned the flames of her curiosity—but she had no reason to pry further. Although Devon's connection was an interesting lead…

"Wait," she said. "If you knew John, will the police want to question you? He wasn't from Driftwood Island, so there aren't many people who would know him here. Unless it was a random murder." She shivered. "And that's even scarier."

"Murders are rarely random," Devon assured her. He paled. "I suppose they might want to question me."

He stared at the body. His brooding silence was interrupted by another Mountie vehicle. Devon excused himself from Brianna and walked over to meet the driver. They exchanged a few words, then Devon entered the passenger's seat. The other Mountie spoke briefly with Lenox, then resettled himself in the vehicle.

Devon gave Brianna a tight nod as the cruiser passed. Brianna bit her lip. Would they really question Devon about John's death, despite him not having seen the dead man for years? Brianna remembered their fraught meeting on the street the other day, and her stomach tightened. Devon and John had had bad blood, and Devon was being cagey about it. What was the real story?

Only Brianna and Lenox were left at the crime scene. Brianna felt pulled in two directions. The crime scene tugged at her, wanting her to notice something about it, but her bakery also called. How had her new batch of spanakopita turned out? Had she cracked the code yet?

She should really head back. She had no reason to involve herself here, and her place was at her business, improving it.

Brianna pulled out her phone. She could settle the pastry issue here, have another quick look at the crime scene, then head back to the Golden Moon. Problem solved.

"Hi, Teri," she said once her employee answered the phone. "It's Brianna. Sorry to bother you. Did you take the spanakopita out of the oven yet?"

"Sure did," she said brightly. "They were practice pastries, right? I might have had a nibble on the edge of one. It was really tasty."

"Better than my usual ones?" Brianna held her breath for Teri's answer.

"It was good, I promise." A rustling sound floated through the speaker, then Teri said, "I need to go. Lots of customers today."

"Of course." Brianna hung up and slid her phone into her purse. What did "really tasty" mean?

She shook her head and hiked her purse higher on her shoulder. The pastries were done, and there was nothing more she could do about them until she returned to the café. For now, she could satisfy her curiosity about the crime scene, then leave.

"You pulled the short straw today?" she said to Lenox. He leaned against the car hood with his arms crossed. His long face looked disgruntled.

"Yeah. Someone needs to guard the crime scene until the coroner and detectives get here. It'll be a few hours yet by the time they catch the ferry. We've already called them here." Lenox peered at her. "How did you end up at another murder site, anyway? You have a nose for this sort of thing?"

"I guess so." Brianna chuckled. "You'll have to blame this one on Macy, though. She was the one who called me here. I have nothing to do with the dead body, not this time."

"Probably for the better." Lenox glanced at the ditch. "This one is pretty sick. Not exactly a crime of passion. Not the way they laid the body out."

"It's almost ritualistic," Brianna said. Lenox seemed more inclined to talk than Devon had been, so she took her opportunity to prod. "Nothing about the setup is random. The feta cheese on the eyes, for instance. Who does that?"

"Feta, hey?" Lenox looked at her with new appreciation. "I guess you'd know, being the cheese queen on the island."

"Is that what they're calling me?" Brianna laughed. "I had no idea."

Lenox stood straighter. "Feta," he said slowly. "Why does that ring a bell?"

"It's a delicious cheese commonly made from sheep or goat's milk, originating from Greece?" Brianna said to trigger his memory.

Lenox snapped his fingers. "Greece, that's it. I was speaking to John's wife Gloria last night in the Stumbling Goose. Well, she cornered me, and I had a hard time getting away." Lenox threw an apologetic glance at the body. "She was relentless. Didn't get much love from her husband, according to her drunken statements. I finally escaped by pleading my need for a smoke break." He leaned forward confidentially. "I don't smoke."

"Smart thinking." Brianna waited for a beat. When Lenox didn't seem poised to continue his story, she prompted him. "Something about Greece?"

"Right, right. Gloria was going on and on about John's research and how much she hated it. He was a journalist, sent to Driftwood Island by his travel magazine, but he had some passion project, some book he wanted to write about Greek crime families and their global connections. A hard-hitting exposé, apparently. Gloria didn't have much time for it. She rambled on and on about how long John was spending on it. But she did mention that some of the crime families, when they execute their enemies, arrange the bodies in ceremonial ways." Lenox stared at the body. "It's a little funny that John's body turned up like this. I wonder if there's a connection."

Brianna stared at the body's blank feta eyes and shivered. Had John's research probed a little too deeply into secrets best left undisturbed?

Her gaze drifted to the vine around John's neck. "Looks like he was strangled."

"We won't know for sure until the coroner's report comes in. But it seems likely. Might have been by that vine, too. It looks like a tough one."

The vine was thick and sturdy-looking without leaves. It wasn't ivy, or clematis, or grape, or any other vine Brianna could name. She looked around. In the closest field, rows of plants supported by long trellises stretched from the road toward a farmhouse beyond. The vines looked suspiciously like the one wrapped around John's neck.

"I'd better get back to work," she said to Lenox. "Good luck with the guarding."

He grunted in acknowledgement and settled against the car hood once more. Brianna swung her leg over the bike and pedaled down the road. At the next driveway, she slowed and looked at the sign with a gulp. "Kiwi Ridge Orchard," painted in white, hung from a fencepost.

John's body was lying in a ditch beside Costas Dimitriou's kiwi farm with what looked like a kiwi vine around his neck. Costas, the kiwi farmer from Greece whom nobody knew much about. Brianna shivered. If she were a detective, he would be the first person she would investigate.

Brianna pedaled resolutely onward. Luckily, she wasn't a detective. Her biggest mystery was solving the riddle of her spanakopita recipe. Her heart squeezed for Costas, who was about to fall under scrutiny. He had seemed like a friendly, pleasant man who Brianna wouldn't wish trouble on. Assuming he hadn't committed murder, of course.

Chapter 4

Brianna rolled into the alley beside the Golden Moon a few minutes later, her cheeks red from the cold air. She locked her bike to the drainpipe and stepped with trepidation into the kitchen. Bustling sounds from the dining area filtered through the open doorway between the rooms, but Brianna had eyes only for the cooling rack full of pastries on the counter. She walked gingerly toward them and picked one up.

The heft was good, and the top layer was a lovely golden brown. Brianna broke off a piece and examined the inside. Flaky layers concealed a luscious green filling dotted with melted cheese nodules. She closed her eyes and placed the morsel on her tongue.

After a few chews, her tense shoulders drooped. Oh, it was fine enough, but it didn't have the sublime quality of the pastry she'd tasted on the ferry. How had they done it? How could she deconstruct that deliciousness and recreate it in her own kitchen?

Brianna took a deep breath to steady herself. More important things were happening in Snuggler's Cove. A man had died, for pity's sake. And she was worrying about baked goods? She shook her head to clear it and donned an apron. If she was going to mope about pastries, she might as well be productive about it and try another tweak of the recipe. After she'd prepared café food for the next day, of course.

After much encouragement from Macy, Brianna had recently introduced two lunch items to the café's usual menu of coffee, tea, and pastries. Macaroni and cheese was an obvious choice, especially since she could make a large batch every few days, portion it out, and have Teri warm each bowl up as needed. For grilled cheese sandwiches, she'd bought a panini press. Pre-assembled sandwiches out of her own cheese bread with slices of cheddar inside cooked up nicely for customers.

So far, the offerings had been a hit. The café was almost out of macaroni and cheese, so Brianna put on a large pot of water to boil and took out the four cheeses she needed to create her own special sauce.

"Hello?" Dot poked her head into the kitchen. "Oh good, you're here. I desperately need a cup of tea."

"You'll have to pull up a stool, I'm afraid." Brianna nodded at her office nook. "I'm happy to chat, but I'm in the middle of cooking."

"Of course." Dot disappeared to the front and returned a few minutes later with a mug of tea. She pulled the stool closer to Brianna and nestled herself onto it. She leaned against the wall with a contented sigh.

"Much better." Raising the mug to her lips, she sipped the liquid. "Just what I needed on a chilly day. What's new with you, my lovely niece?"

"I just came back from a murder site." Brianna stirred the melting butter in her saucepan. "You know, as one does."

"What?" Dot sat upright and stared at her. "What are you talking about?"

"Macy called me this morning. She found a body in a

ditch on the side of the road. It was a man named John Albright, some journalist who'd come to write a travel piece about Driftwood Island."

"That's terrible."

Brianna scooped flour into her melted butter to make a roux, then splashed milk in and stirred. "You haven't heard the strangest part. He was laid out in the ditch with his arms crossed, as if in preparation for a viewing. And someone had placed slices of feta cheese on his eyes."

Dot blinked at Brianna, her forehead creased in a frown. "What are you saying?"

"I don't know." Brianna shrugged, her mind working. "Ritualistic killing points to premeditated murder. This was no accident."

"Who was this man? Who had it in for him?"

Brianna put grated cheese into her thickened milk sauce by the handful. Cheddar for color, Asiago for sharpness, gruyere for meltability, and cream cheese for creaminess. She resisted testing for flavor, despite the temptation.

"Macy found him outside Costas Dimitriou's kiwi farm," she said finally. "And the dead man had a kiwi vine around his neck. It doesn't look good for Costas."

Dot clasped a hand to her mouth, eyes wide. "No," she whispered. "That's ridiculous. Someone set Costas up."

"Maybe," Brianna agreed. "I hope so because he seems like a nice guy. But I'm not always a great judge of character."

"You can't blame yourself for dating the wrong men," Dot said sternly. "Bad apples are hard to spot."

"It's true," Brianna agreed. "And that means I can't trust my gut with Costas. John Albright was researching Greek crime families on the side—some passion project of his—and the way the body was laid out is just like how some of them deal with bodies."

Dot's mouth thinned.

"All I'm saying is that it doesn't look good for the kiwi farmer," Brianna finished.

"They'll have to investigate him, for sure." Dot stared at her tea with a look of distaste, although Brianna was sure the beverage wasn't the culprit. Dot looked up at Brianna with narrowed eyes. "But I'm sure Costas is innocent."

"I hope so." Brianna poured cheese sauce onto her drained pasta and stirred. "I was looking forward to eating more kiwis in the future."

The next evening, Brianna walked through the darkness of a blustery late November evening toward the community hall. Wind whipped off the ocean with a piercing keenness that snuck under the hem of her raincoat and filtered through the fabric of her jeans. She shivered and tucked her head deeper into her hood. Trees swayed overhead, and occasional branches dropped with a crack and a thud on the pavement. The single streetlight on this stretch of road flickered but held firm.

Brianna swallowed. Would they lose power tonight? She'd received a quote for solar panels to light up her float home in a power outage, but she hadn't yet ordered them. Her café was doing well, but running a restaurant was never a lucrative business.

She regretted her hesitation when the streetlight flickered again. Dot had mentioned that when the island lost power, they often did without for days, waiting for the power company to travel from the mainland to fix the broken wire. At least her cat Paprika wouldn't mind the darkness.

Brianna walked briskly to the lit porch of the community hall and hurried inside. She pushed the door shut against the wind threatening to blow it inward. When calm descended, she sighed with relief. Her coat joined others on hooks against the wall of the entryway, then she entered the double doors to the main hall.

A solitary folding table sat squarely in the center of the otherwise empty room. The rest of the Gourmand Society clustered around it. Brianna hurried forward, annoyed at herself for being late. Her annoyance faded when Magnus's bushy eyebrows nearly joined as he glared at her. He was annoyed enough for them both, so she didn't need to bother with the emotion.

"Brianna, dear." Hilda Button paused her sock-darning for a moment to pat the chair next to her. Today's sock was lurid green with a fluorescent yellow border. "Have a seat. Isn't it miserable outside? It's brewing up a storm, that's for sure."

"Miserable?" Esme Alonso threw up her chin. Her dangling gold earrings glittered in the overhead light with faceted blue gems that complemented her vibrant eyeshadow and drifting silk scarf. "All in the eye of the beholder. It's wild and full of life and excitement. Stirs up the blood."

"Do you really need more stirring?" Quentin Flagstaff said, his mouth prim. He straightened the papers in front of him with a fussy motion. Even his bowtie was perfectly in line.

"Everyone could use more stirring, darling." Esme winked at Brianna.

Brianna grinned back and sat next to Hilda. She agreed with Esme. The wind, although it brought power outages and destruction, was also fierce and thrilling. She enjoyed having her breath taken away by powerful gusts. As long as she had a snug home to retreat to.

"That's enough of that." Magnus made harrumphing noises, then glared at them all. "To business. As we all know, our Christmas potluck is only a couple of weeks away. Hilda, would you like to delegate duties to the society?"

"Of course," Hilda said with a satisfied gleam in her eyes.

"Wait." Brianna tilted her head in question. "What Christmas potluck?"

"Every year, the Gourmand Society hosts a community dinner," said Quentin. "Anyone who lives on the island can come, as long as they bring a dish to share."

"We had to dig out the extra tables last year," Esme said. "It was popular."

"Of course it was," Magnus declared. "It's the center point of our community's calendar."

"Let me see." Hilda rested her hands on the table,

momentarily forgetting to darn her sock in her concentration. "Someone will need to organize volunteers to help set up and take down. That had better be you, Quentin. Magnus, you can put up flyers to advertise around town, remind people of the date. Esme, you did such a splendid job of finding entertainment last year. That guitarist was quite lovely. Why don't you take on that role again?"

"Bernardo won't be available this year." Esme tapped her fingers on the table in thought. "But I'm sure I can come up with something."

"What can I do?" Brianna asked. Christmas felt like a long time away, but she knew it would arrive before long. Her previous Christmas had been soaked in the shock and sadness of her husband's death. She was looking forward to a fresh start this year.

"We have a Santa Claus costume," Hilda said proudly. "You can find someone to dress up and hand out goodies for the children. Joe Hicks used to do it, but he passed away last February, poor soul."

Brianna stared at Hilda. Who did she know who would suit the role of Santa? She wondered if Magnus would trade jobs. She dismissed that thought. He would probably dress up as Santa himself and scare the children with his gruffness.

"I'll do my best," Brianna promised. She had a few weeks to find someone. Maybe Dot would have a suggestion.

"Speaking of Christmas"—Hilda wagged her finger at Brianna—"I noticed you haven't decorated your café yet. December comes in two days, you know. All the other shops have been dressed up for ages."

"Did you see the display at the salon?" Esme said. "Tinsel everywhere, and the cutest inflatable squirrel with a Santa hat on. They're in the spirit, that's for sure."

"It felt too early," Brianna protested. "December first, I'll get some things up, I promise."

"I suppose that will have to do." Hilda heaved a sigh and picked up her sock again. "We take the holidays seriously around here."

Brianna, chastised, turned to Magnus. He saved her from Hilda's Christmas scolding by changing the subject.

"Any food-related news on Driftwood Island? We need to keep abreast of important happenings."

"The Silver Spoon bistro introduced a beef Wellington dish that's truly excellent," Quentin said. Brightened eyes enlivened his normally calm demeanor. "It has a savory flavor and delectable richness that's worth visiting for. I suggest pairing it with a bold merlot."

Brianna's mind wandered to her spanakopita. Would people ever speak about it like Quentin had the beef Wellington?

The pastry suggested feta cheese, which reminded Brianna of John's death with an unpleasant jolt.

"I have news that's sort of food related," she said once Quentin and the others had finished discussing the Silver Spoon's newest dish. "Did you hear about the murder yesterday?"

"I hardly think that's relevant to the Gourmand Society," Magnus huffed. "The man was a journalist. Nothing to do with food."

"Journalists can write about food." Esme shot Magnus a raised eyebrow. "I write plenty of restaurant critiques for magazines."

Magnus waved away her objection. "But the murder victim wasn't writing about food."

"He was doing a travel piece on Driftwood and the surrounding islands," Hilda piped up. Her hands stilled on the green sock in her excitement to be spreading gossip. "His name was John Albright. My daughter Rosy met him a few days ago. He and his wife Gloria were staying at the Bumblebee, along with their photographer Sam Brown."

"Now we know the murder victim's name and occupation," Magnus said with an aggrieved sigh. "But I still don't see why the Gourmand Society should be interested. Where is the food?"

"I saw the body," Brianna said. "My friend Macy Jones discovered it. And it was carefully laid out like at a funeral. On each eye was placed a slice of feta cheese."

Silence greeted this declaration. All eyes were on Brianna. She suppressed a chuckle at their fascination.

"I heard they found the body in the ditch outside of Costas Dimitriou's kiwi farm," Quentin said in a hushed tone.

"Maybe the killer grabbed a nearby kiwi vine to strangle John with, because there was one wrapped around his neck." Brianna clasped her hands in front of her on the table.

"You don't think they'll go after Costas?" Hilda said. "Oh my, how terrible. He's such a lovely young man. Quiet, but he always offers me a ride at the car stop if I need it."

"And handsome, too." Esme wiggled her eyebrows. "I would hate to think of that good-looking face hiding a killer personality."

Quentin shot Esme a glare at her terrible pun, but she only grinned and leaned back in her chair.

Brianna swallowed. Poor Costas. It was so easy to point fingers at him. Was he truly the killer? She found it hard to believe of the mild-mannered man she'd met at the market.

"That's strange about the cheese on the eyes." Now that the murder had something to do with food, Magnus was as eager as anyone else to discuss it. "Why would the killer do that?"

"Like coins on the eyes to pay the ferryman," Esme said. "Maybe the afterlife guardian is tired of money and wants a savory bite instead."

"Esme," Quentin said with exasperation. "Whatever happened to respecting the dead?"

"Did you meet him?" Esme crossed her arms. "I bumped into John Albright at the Apple Cart. He nearly bowled me over, then had the gall to yell at me. Me! I don't let myself be shouted at, let me tell you, so I gave him a piece of my mind. He got so angry that he practically spat at me."

"He didn't treat my daughter Rosy well at all," Hilda agreed with a nod. "Demanding and obnoxious. He and his wife left their room each morning in a right state for the poor cleaners, too. We were counting the days until they left."

"He interviewed me about the marina," Magnus

chipped in. His eyebrows nearly met in the middle with his frown. "For his magazine article about the island. It felt like an interrogation. Wouldn't take my answers as they were, kept prodding for details and secrets that weren't there. I finally kicked him out of the marina office, but he skulked around the boats for another half-hour with that photographer chap."

"He left Zinnia at the candy shop nearly in tears with his questions," Hilda said. Her lips tightened. "Tried to show her in a poor light."

"I have the feeling he was trying for a damning exposé of the island, not a travel guide," Esme said with a knowing nod. "I'm sorry that someone murdered him— nobody deserves that—but at least he won't show the island in such a negative way."

"Undeservedly so," Magnus huffed. "Driftwood Island is the jewel in the Gulf Islands' crown. Anyone who doesn't see that is blind."

Brianna understood Magnus's devotion. She was feeling it herself for her new home. Six months she'd been living here, and it already felt like a comfortable second skin.

"But it's time to move on from gruesome news." Magnus drew himself up in his chair. "It's unfortunate timing, but I'd already planned a discussion around feta cheese, and I'm not about to change it just because some sicko desecrated a few slices. Quentin? Did you bring the samples?"

Quentin brought out a tub of freshly cut feta. The briny, sour scent traveled across the table, and Brianna breathed deeply. The motivations of murderers were hard to understand, but cheese made the world make sense again.

Chapter 5

Brianna rang Macy's townhouse's doorbell the next evening. The flowerpot that had held bright chrysanthemums a few months ago was now empty with the onslaught of freezing nights and bitter winds. Brianna stamped her feet for warmth as she waited for the door to open. The doorway's paint was peeling in spots, and the wind pushed the neighbor's creaky gate back and forth. But orange light from the window spilled onto the scraggly front lawn with a welcoming glow.

Finally, the door swung open.

"Get in here." Macy pulled Brianna inside. "It's way too cold out there. Come in and warm up."

Brianna gratefully stepped inside and sniffed at a savory scent permeating the house. Macy slammed the door shut behind her and rubbed her hands together.

"I brought buns like you asked." Brianna held out her tin of baking and Macy took it.

"Cheese, I hope?" At Brianna's nod, Macy smiled. "I expected nothing less. Why don't you pop your coat in the closet and come into the kitchen. I think the chicken is almost done."

Brianna found room in the overstuffed hall closet and walked the few steps through Macy's living room. It contained a tweed patterned couch, its aging fabric covered by a carefully tucked-in throw blanket. A small television sat on a chipped console table against the wall.

Bright paintings from Oaklyn's childhood art projects were framed and hung on the walls in pride of place.

Brianna reached Macy's diminutive kitchen at the back of the house. She placed a bottle of wine on the crowded counter. "Can I help?"

"No, it's fine." Macy glanced around the mayhem in the kitchen. Dishes crowded the sink, and cutting boards and vegetables sprawled over the counters. "Well, maybe you could finish putting together the salad."

Brianna washed her hands at the sink and grabbed a knife to continue Macy's work with a carrot. Macy peered into the oven. "I think it's almost done," she said with glee. "Let me check."

She pulled out the roast chicken with a folded tea towel and dropped it on the stove. She poked the bird with a thermometer. Her shoulders drooped.

"Not yet." Macy sighed. "And now I've let all the heat out of the oven, and we'll have to wait even longer for it to cook. I'm terrible at cooking chicken!"

She slapped the tea towel against her leg and gave a shuddering sigh.

"It will be fine. We're in no rush." Brianna took the tea towel from her distraught friend and slid the tray back in the oven. Once the door closed, she turned to Macy. "Okay, now spill. What's up? You don't normally throw your hands up over a silly chicken."

"Everything's fine." Macy turned to the counter and picked up a carrot, but she did nothing with it.

Brianna touched her shoulder. "Come on, you can tell me. Get it off your chest."

Macy heaved a sigh and glanced at Brianna with

expressive eyes. "It's Costas," she whispered. "I'm so worried for him."

Brianna blinked. Where did all this emotion come from?

"Costas Dimitriou, the kiwi farmer." Brianna wanted to make perfectly clear who they were talking about. "That's who you're worried about?"

"Yes." Macy took a vegetable peeler off the counter and held it in a limp hand. "That body I found? It was right outside his farm. The police are questioning him. It's horrible."

Brianna frowned. "I know you're a lovely, empathetic person, but you're taking this way harder than I expected."

"Costas is Oaklyn's badminton coach." Macy bit her lip. "He's been so great for her, really propping her up, getting her to reach new heights. Now, the police are questioning him. We're both so worried about him."

Brianna still wondered about the depths of Macy's anxiety, but she let it slide. If Macy wanted to tell her something, she would do it in her own time. Well, Brianna might prod a little further, but she could drop it for this moment.

"The body had a kiwi vine wrapped around its neck, maybe strangled by it," Brianna said. "And the dead man, John Albright, came after Costas in the market, asking about his Greek heritage. Apparently, John was writing a book about Greek crime families. Some of them left their kills in distinctive positions, just like how we found John's body, with the arms and the cheese just so." Brianna winced at Macy's stricken expression. "All I'm saying is that it doesn't look good for Costas. How well do you know him?"

Macy's teenage daughter Oaklyn burst into the kitchen, her black-lined eyes wide with horror and anger. "Costas would never do something like that. You don't know him at all. There's no way he's a killer."

"I'm sorry you had to hear that, Oaklyn." Brianna glanced at Macy with apology. "And I'm not saying Costas did it, just that it looks bad for him."

Oaklyn burst into tears and ran from the room. Macy raced after her.

Brianna sighed and peeked through the oven's window. The chicken wasn't burning yet, so she left it to come up to temperature while she chopped vegetables for their salad. She'd forgotten that Oaklyn was likely within earshot in this little duplex. She wasn't used to tiptoeing around kids.

Macy returned, and Brianna spoke quickly. "I'm sorry I said that where Oaklyn could hear it. I didn't mean to upset her."

"It's fine." Macy leaned against the counter, looking drained. "She would have heard it somewhere. Better here, where she can get the first shock out of her system without bawling at school or somewhere more embarrassing for her."

"She seems really concerned about Costas."

"Like I said, he's her badminton coach." Macy grabbed a piece of cucumber and crunched it between her teeth. "He's taken the team from last in the league to first in the islands. The kids adore him for that. And he's great at motivating them. I've watched a practice or two, and he pushes them hard but only to the point of growth, you know? They all feel on top of the world after practice, no being bullied around. He's a bit of a family friend, now."

Macy said this last sentence in a mumble. Brianna narrowed her eyes.

"Family friend?" she repeated. At Macy's nod, Brianna stared at her. "Is that all?"

Macy colored. "He's a good guy," she murmured to the floor. When she caught Brianna's eyes, she tossed her head defiantly. "Fine, I like him. He's kind, and sweet, and he likes birdwatching almost as much as I do. I want to get to know him better. Happy?"

Brianna grinned. "That wasn't so hard to admit, was it?"

Macy's answering smile drooped into a frown almost before it began. "But now he's under suspicion for murder." She gazed with pleading eyes at Brianna. "I swear, there's no way it can be him. I couldn't bear it if he were a killer."

Brianna swallowed hard. She knew exactly how Macy felt. Brianna had had experience with wonderful, caring men who turned out to be liars in the worst way. She didn't want Macy near anything like that.

"Surely that chicken is done by now." Macy turned and opened the oven door. She pulled the tray out with the folded tea towel and placed it on the stove. With a triumphant flourish of her thermometer, she said, "Yes! Now we can eat. Oaklyn! Dinner's ready."

Brianna brought the salad and her tin of cheese buns to the tiny kitchen table. Oaklyn slouched in with reddened eyes and pushed an ottoman from the living room toward the table as a third seat. With a satisfied sigh, Macy placed the chicken in the center of the table.

"There we are. Finally, the chicken is done. Here, let me slice some pieces off for everyone."

They dug into the meal. Oaklyn had less gusto than the others, but she still took a bun with a swift grab when Brianna offered her one. The chicken was slightly on the dry side, but with a side helping of chutney, the buttery roasted flavors shone through.

"What if the killer strikes again?" Oaklyn said in a lull in the conversation. "They were deranged enough to put cheese on the body's eyes. They could come after anyone."

"According to Corporal Moore, murders are rarely random," Brianna said with a glance at Macy.

"Some whack job on the loose makes way more sense than Costas having done it." Oaklyn stabbed a piece of chicken with an aggressive poke of her fork. "It's too creepy. Kind of scary. And we live alone here. Our back door doesn't even lock properly, half the time."

Oaklyn's face grew paler as she chewed. Was she considering the killer loose on the streets of Snuggler's Cove?

Macy looked disquieted. "I'm sure the killer had a connection to the dead man," she said, but her own drawn features spoke otherwise.

Brianna sipped her wine and studied her friend. For their own peace of mind, Macy and Oaklyn needed to know who had killed John Albright. A random killer roaming Driftwood Island seemed highly unlikely, but the notion was affecting these two.

And Macy deserved to know the truth about Costas. Brianna couldn't bear it if Macy developed further feelings for a man who lied to her. She deserved better than that.

Brianna sighed and picked apart her cheese bun. Once again, a mystery had dropped in her lap. And with Devon unable to aid the detectives on this case—given that he was too close to the victim—Brianna didn't trust that they would gather all the information they needed to find the true killer.

If Brianna could help, then she needed to do so, for Macy and Oaklyn's sake.

Brianna wanted to talk about the case with Devon, but Hilda had bustled into the café yesterday with the news that he was on administrative leave. He wouldn't know what was going on with the investigation. Anyway, he would likely tell her not to look into it, as he always did. She would have to do without his insights for now.

What she could do was find out who might have bought feta cheese recently. The pieces laid on John Albright's eyes might be the smoking gun that Brianna needed. While Teri managed the front of the Golden Moon, and Brianna was waiting on her bread in the oven, she picked up her phone and dialed the grocery store.

After two rings, a chipper female voice answered. "This is the Apple Cart. How can I help you today?"

"Good morning," Brianna answered. "This is a

random question, but do you recall who might have bought feta cheese in the past week?"

"Umm…" The woman sounded confused.

Brianna didn't blame her. She held her breath and waited for an answer.

"We get a lot of customers through here," the woman said finally. "I'm really sorry, but we don't track that information."

"Understandable. Thanks, anyway. Do you know who else on the island might sell feta cheese?"

The woman paused, considering. "Isn't there that goat farm on the south end? I think we get our feta cheese from them. Some of it, anyway."

Brianna thanked her and hung up. After a quick search on her phone for the goat farm, she dialed another number.

"Yep," a gruff male voice answered.

"Is this Grant's Goats?" Brianna asked.

"Yep."

"A friend of mine brought some feta cheese to a party a couple of days ago. It was delicious, and I'm trying to track down where he bought it. He's out of cell range right now, unfortunately." Brianna chided herself for spinning the lie out. Best to keep it simple. "Do you remember who you sold your feta cheese to this week?"

"We don't sell to the public," the man said brusquely. "Only commercial. Better ask at the store."

Brianna signed off with a sigh. Following the cheese trail had taken her nowhere. It was time to gather gossip.

Brianna pedaled up a side road close to Snuggler's Cove once her bread was out of the oven and the rest of her morning baking lined the display case in the Golden Moon. She'd used the kiwis purchased from the market last week in a new treat to prepare for this afternoon's visit. As Macy always said, the best way to butter up a suspect was with plenty of butter.

She wheeled into a gravel driveway that traveled up a shallow incline from the road. Farms dotted the landscape on either side. A small farmhouse stood at the end of the driveway, with an ancient-looking barn behind it. Barren kiwi vines twined around trellises that ran in tidy rows from the road to well past the barn. Before she could wonder whether she should knock on the door, a familiar figure walked between barns.

"Yoo hoo," Brianna called. "Costas Dimitriou?"

Costas whirled around. His face opened in a genuine smile when he recognized Brianna, and he strode toward her. She flicked open her kickstand to rest her bicycle on the driveway.

"Hello," he said, when he was close enough to speak at a normal volume. "From the last market day, right?"

"Brianna West." She stuck out her hand, and he shook it. "I'm the owner of the Golden Moon cheese café in Snuggler's Cove. I was hoping to speak to you about your kiwis."

"Of course. Would you like to come in from the cold?"

Costas ushered her onto the porch of a tiny farmhouse with white clapboard siding. The porch held a painted bench, handmade by the looks of it, and led to a Dutch door with window paneling in the top half. It was painted a cheery yellow.

Costas held the door open for her, and Brianna entered the small space inside. Oak floors that desperately needed sanding lined the hallway. A bright opening at the end beckoned Brianna into a well-lit kitchen with a small table. Dishes piled in the sink, but the scent of fresh toast lingered in the air with a pleasant aroma. A window beside the table overlooked rows of kiwi plants on trellises.

"Please, sit." Costas grabbed two mismatched mugs from a cupboard and splashed coffee into each one from a metal carafe on the stove.

Brianna wrapped her cold hands around the hot mug Costas gave her and sipped it gratefully. "This is lovely. These overnight freezes are getting through my mittens."

"I can't complain. That frost ripened my kiwis," Costas replied.

Brianna opened her baking tin and presented it to the kiwi farmer. He picked out a treat with eager fingers.

"They're mini kiwi cheesecakes," she explained. "I'm considering making them to sell at my café when kiwis are in season, and I was hoping you'd be interested in selling me some fruit every week when it's ripe. Do you sell all your produce to the Apple Cart, or do you have some that is looking for a home?"

"Absolutely." Costas's face shone. "I do deliveries on Mondays. How many would you like? I can only offer fresh fruit until February, maybe March."

"That's great. I'll work out the details and get back to

you on numbers." Brianna nodded at the dessert in Costas's hand. "What do you think? Does it showcase your kiwis adequately?"

Costas took a bite and chewed with a contented smile on his face. "Delicious," he said finally. "And such a great color."

They chatted a little more about the café and life on the island, then Brianna drained her cup.

"I'd love to see your kiwi vines." She hadn't been able to turn the conversation toward her goals yet. She needed a little more time and opportunity. "I've only seen them from a distance."

"Yes, please, follow me." He leaped up and bounded to the door.

Costas chatted happily about the vines as they walked down the rows. He pointed out where kiwis had hung in fat clusters before harvesting, places where he'd pruned, the first vines he'd planted and the most recent, and every detail that came into his head.

Finally, Brianna steered the conversation toward John Albright's murder. She wasn't as tactful at changing subjects as Macy was, but she did the best she could.

"It must have been a shock to have that journalist murdered in your front yard." Brianna gave Costas a sympathetic look.

Costas nodded somberly. "Just terrible. That poor man."

"He was a bit of a bear toward you at the market."

"That's right, you were there." Costas shrugged. "He was rude, yes. But I'm sure his family must be missing him."

"I suppose." His wife had seemed as obnoxious as John, but maybe that was why they suited one another. "I heard the police are looking into his murder. Have they bothered you yet?"

"Yes." Costas frowned and pulled a kiwi vine closer to his face to inspect an end. "They think because I live here that I might have done it. Oh, and because I'm Greek."

"Greek?" Brianna tilted her head in question to get Costas to explain further. She wanted to know what he would say about the subject, uninfluenced by her. "What does that have to do with anything?"

"Apparently, the man, John, was researching Greek families." Costas scowled. "And now he is dead in front of my farm. But I had nothing to do with it. I wasn't even alone at the time."

"Who were you with?" An alibi would be invaluable for exonerating Costas.

"Do you know Macy Jones? She was over that evening."

Brianna blinked. Macy hadn't mentioned that little tidbit. A family friend, indeed.

"Yes, Macy is a close friend of mine." She sighed theatrically. "I wonder who would do such a terrible thing. Murder, on our sleepy little island!"

"It's usually the wife, isn't it?" Costas released the kiwi vine, and they walked toward the driveway and Brianna's bicycle. "In stories, anyway. And she would know all about John's Greek obsession. Maybe she set the whole thing up to put the police off her trail."

"Maybe," Brianna said noncommittally. Gloria

Albright was certainly worth examining further, but Costas's reasoning was weak. She would have to check with Macy to confirm Costas's alibi. But why hadn't Macy mentioned her visit before now?

Chapter 6

Brianna said goodbye to Costas after arranging a delivery of kiwis to the Golden Moon for the next Monday. The mystery of Macy's visit to Costas lurked in her mind, and she pedaled directly to Happy Hearts preschool. Wind buffeted her body and slowed her progress to a crawl. Brianna breathed deeply, the cool air a balm on her warm cheeks.

She wheeled into the preschool's driveway and leaned her bike against the wall mural of squirrels and butterflies. She texted Macy, then browsed a pharmacy across the street for Christmas decorations while she waited. The shop hardly had anything left, and Brianna's heart sank. How was she supposed to decorate the Golden Moon sufficiently? Annalise at the yarn shop next door to her had already festooned her window with tinsel and figurines. Brianna had nothing, since this was her first Christmas as a café owner. Even her personal decorations were sparse, as she'd downsized during her move to the island, and her late husband hadn't been big into the holiday season, anyway.

She bought the last tinsel garland the shop had and tucked it under her arm. Macy was waiting for her at the preschool, her hands in her pockets and her hood pulled up over her head.

"I only have a fifteen-minute break, and I want to grab a coffee in that time," Macy said in greeting. "Come walk with me."

Brianna fell into place beside Macy's vigorous stride.

"I heard you visited Costas the evening before the murder." Brianna didn't beat around the bush. They had limited time, and Macy wouldn't be offended. "I thought he was just Oaklyn's coach, but there's something more going on, isn't there?"

Macy's cheeks flushed from more than the brisk wind. "Don't be mad that I didn't tell you," she said in a rush. "It's just that it's been so long since I've dated anyone. I almost don't feel like it's real. I didn't want to jinx myself."

Brianna tucked her hand into the crook of Macy's arm. "You silly goof. Of course I'm not mad. I'm happy for you. How long have you been dating?"

"Hardly any time at all, but it's going really well. Four dates so far, maybe? Oaklyn knows about it, and she's not putting up too much fuss, which shows how much she likes Costas. And yes, he invited me over to his place for dinner that evening."

"And you stayed the night?"

Macy scoffed. "No! We're not there yet. What would I say to Oaklyn? No, we just had dinner and a nice evening. He made souvlaki. I left by ten."

Brianna sighed. "Too bad. I was really hoping that you would be Costas's airtight alibi for John's murder. But if you left at the end of the evening, Costas still had all night to kill John."

Macy tore her arm away from Brianna's and whirled to face her. Her expression was aghast. "You're not seriously considering that Costas is the killer? There's no way."

"I need to look at everyone objectively."

"I promise Costas is fine." Macy crossed her arms and glared at Brianna. "Sometimes we need to trust our gut feelings."

"I'd be remiss if I ignored clues just because you're dating him."

"Fine." Macy looked away. "Here's the coffee shop. I'll talk to you later."

Macy turned on the spot and marched through the coffee shop's glass door. Brianna stared after her friend, her mind reeling. Was she looking too closely at Costas?

No, she decided. Too many clues pointed in his direction, and she would be foolish to ignore them based on a character reference alone. She hoped Macy would forgive her in time. After all, she wanted Costas exonerated for Macy and Oaklyn's sake, but only if he was innocent.

Brianna pedaled back to the café, her mind reeling from her disagreement with Macy. She needed to solve this mystery soon, or at least cross Costas off the suspect list, so she could repair her relationship with her closest friend. Driftwood Island would be a much less welcoming place for her without Macy.

Teri was still holding down the fort at the café when Brianna arrived. She washed up, examined the display case for any baked goods they were low on, and got to baking. She couldn't resist trying another spanakopita recipe. The perfect spinach-feta pastry was within her reach, she knew it.

After an hour, she emerged at the sound of Devon Moore's voice in the dining room. She'd been wanting to catch up with him ever since the murder scene.

"I can take over, Teri," she said. "If you want to bring the fresh baking to the display case."

"What's fresh?" Devon asked.

"A new spanakopita recipe I'm trying."

"I'll take one."

"Not your usual scone assortment? It's a bit late in the day for that, maybe."

"I'm on leave at the moment." Devon's face darkened briefly. "Sergeant thought it would be best."

"Because you and John Albright knew each other?" Brianna frowned. "I thought the detectives took care of investigations."

"We're often tasked with helping them." Devon shrugged and didn't meet Brianna's eye. "And I'm under suspicion. I'm on leave while they investigate."

"Just a single spanakopita, then." Brianna rang up his purchase and slid the pastry into a takeaway bag. She didn't want to pry further into what was clearly a sensitive topic, but her need for information prevailed. "How did you know John Albright, anyway? I thought he was from Vancouver."

"He is." Devon passed Brianna some cash. "We were in cadet training together, in Saskatchewan."

Brianna dropped coins in the till. "Classmate rivals, then?"

"Rivals?" He squinted at her. "No, I had nothing

against John. He was ambitious, with a quick temper, but I mostly stayed out of his way, his and his wife's. Well, she was his girlfriend at the time. They got together that first year. I don't know how they stuck together for so long when it only started as an infatuation."

"Maybe money was involved?" Brianna suggested.

"She came with plenty of it. And she's Catholic and firmly against divorce."

"They didn't seem like a very close couple," Brianna said as delicately as she could muster. John and Gloria had been practically screaming at each other at the market, and in the brief interlude she'd seen them together, they hadn't shown a single iota of affection toward each other.

"Like I said, I don't know how they stuck together for so long. When they hooked up, I gave them a year, max." Devon picked up his coffee and blew on the surface to cool it. "She was probably savvy enough to get a pre-nuptial agreement for her assets. She came from money. If John wanted to keep himself in his accustomed lifestyle, he would have had to stick around. Honestly, if I were at the detachment, I would advise looking into Gloria as a culprit."

"I thought you said she was a staunch Catholic. Don't they rather disapprove of murder?"

"There's a difference between a crime of passion and drawn-out divorce proceedings. And with John gone, Gloria could move on from the marriage without issue."

"But the killer laid John out like a funeral, hardly the result of a crime of passion."

"The murderer could have arranged the body after the

act, once remorse or a cooler head prevailed." Devon shook his head. "Look at me, gossiping like the rest of them. That's what happens when I get a few days off. Terrible."

Brianna chuckled and passed him his change. "Welcome to the rest of the island. Gossip is the primary currency around here."

Devon narrowed his eyes at her. "You're not investigating John's demise, are you? I know I asked you before, but I'm getting a strong sense that you're prodding for information."

Brianna ran her hands over the counter edge, not making eye contact. Devon worried about her. It was sweet, but she wasn't about to stop investigating because of it.

"I'm simply curious," she said. "It's a big event that happened in our sleepy town."

"Be careful." Devon bent his head until Brianna met his searching gaze. His warm brown eyes peered at her. "I'm not at the detachment these days. I can't be there to smooth things over if it gets rough for you. Not every detective is as pleased with local interference as the last two were."

"I'm just curious," Brianna repeated. She glanced at a customer approaching from behind Devon.

He turned his head to follow her gaze, then backed away to give the woman room.

"Take care, Brianna," he said again and retreated from the café.

Brianna stared after Devon. He'd given her food for thought. She hated to think ill of the Mountie who had always been kind and supportive toward her, but his answers about his connection to John rang false. The two had more history than Devon was letting on. And Brianna had forgotten to ask his whereabouts during the night of the murder.

Truthfully, she hadn't wanted to ask. He would have seen through her seemingly innocent questions in a heartbeat for what they really were—an interrogation—and she wasn't ready to wound their friendship like that. Not yet, anyway. She needed far more evidence supporting his involvement before she traveled that path. She was already on shaky ground with Macy.

The new customer before her cleared her throat. Brianna jumped and hitched on a smile.

"What can I get for you today?"

Two people had pointed to Gloria Albright as a suspect, and it was time to meet her in person. Brianna thought hard about the best way to approach the woman all afternoon at the café and well into the evening at her float home. It wasn't until she was sitting on her couch stroking Paprika's purring back with her phone in the other hand that she found inspiration.

She'd been perusing a chat group set up for residents of Driftwood Island, idly curious about what events might come up for Christmas. Quentin had posted the Gourmand Society's community dinner multiple times already. The announcements were interspersed with offers of firewood for sale, a notice for yoga classes, and an ad for an aluminum dinghy.

Brianna flicked her thumb upward and yawned. She should get to bed shortly if she wanted to be awake bright and early for baking. A different announcement caught her eye, and she blinked to clear the sleepiness from her gaze.

It was an invitation to a celebration of life for John Albright. Brianna read further. Someone had organized a wake for the man to take place tomorrow afternoon at the community hall, even though he wasn't a local. How curious.

Brianna leaned her head back and contemplated the ceiling. As far as she knew, Gloria Albright was still on the island dealing with the aftermath of her husband's death and the investigation surrounding it. Surely, she would attend her own husband's wake. She might even be the one organizing it, although why she would host one here when the couple weren't islanders was hard to comprehend.

Brianna nodded, gave Paprika one last scratch behind the ears, then gently stood up. If she was baking and interrogating suspects tomorrow, she definitely needed her brain sharp and ready.

Chapter 7

Once the café was in its sleepy afternoon lull, Brianna hung up her apron and changed into suitably somber clothes in the café's bathroom. Oaklyn presided over the dining room, but she barely spoke to her employer. Brianna sighed and hitched her purse farther up her shoulder on her way out the door. Oaklyn was still smarting from Brianna's suspicion of her beloved badminton coach. At least the emotional teenager had turned up for work and wasn't treating the customers with the same reticence she showed her boss.

Brianna pedaled slowly through the village of Snuggler's Cove. The wind was finally still, and a heavy fog had rolled in. Sweeping conifers on the edge of town played peek-a-boo in the drifting clouds, and a muffled stillness had fallen over the water. Even the waves in the bay held a muted quality to their crashing. A raven chortled and croaked from some unseen height as it flew past.

Brianna soaked it all up. She adored Snuggler's Cove in the summer sun, with its dazzling waters and cheery ice cream vendor umbrellas dotting the edge. But there was something magical about a foggy day on the west coast. The fog settled over the land like a comfortable blanket, as if the trees had been naked in the summer sun and now were exactly how they wanted to be.

Cars filled the small gravel parking lot beside

Snuggler's Cove community hall when Brianna rode up. She dismounted and leaned her bicycle against the side of the building with her helmet dangling from the handlebars.

Past the hall's entryway, where Brianna hung her coat on a hook, several people milled around a table of food, and more chatted in the center of the room. The crowd was larger than Brianna had expected, given that few on the island had known the deceased. Enough gossip mongers and free-food imbibers had turned up to fill out the gathering.

Gloria Albright stood, apart and aloof, at one side of a bulletin board on wheels. Hilda Button chatted with animation to a stocky, middle-aged man with wispy brown hair, a pregnant woman with her black hair in a pixie cut above an elfin face dabbed her eyes while Magnus Pickleton crunched a carrot next to her, and many other people she didn't recognize conversed quietly to each other.

Brianna took a plate and a few appetizers from a platter clearly purchased from the Apple Cart grocery store. She waved at Hilda when the older woman acknowledged her with a cheery greeting, but she didn't engage in conversation yet. The purpose of her visit was standing at the bulletin board, and she wanted to grab the bull by the horns. Answers awaited her.

"Hello, I'm Brianna West." Brianna stuck her hand out as she approached Gloria. "I'm so sorry for your loss."

Gloria stared down her nose at the offered hand for long enough that Brianna wondered whether to pull it back. Finally, Gloria grasped it in an unenthusiastic handshake.

"Gloria Albright." She swallowed and blinked rapidly.

"It was a terrible tragedy," Brianna said with a sympathetic nod. "Just horrible. I was with the woman who found your husband, and I wanted to pay my condolences today. I understand how devastating it can be."

"It's been hard." Gloria's voice was raspy, possibly from recent crying or maybe from lack of sleep. She blinked again and dabbed at her eyes, although they were dry.

"My husband died suddenly last year." Brianna smiled sadly. "Killed during a stakeout gone wrong. He was a detective. It throws your whole life upside down in an instant."

"Exactly." Gloria stared at Brianna with more appreciation than before, perhaps recognizing a kindred spirit. She rubbed a gold cross pendant hanging from a fine chain around her neck. "Honestly, I should have known something like this was coming. He was obsessed with that crime family research. It was only a matter of time before it caught up to him."

"Obsessed? That must have been hard to deal with, as his spouse." Brianna hoped she wasn't lathering on the sympathetic vibe too thick, but Gloria leaned forward.

"You have no idea. Every second conversation was about his book, the information he was digging up, where he could travel next to find out more, who he could talk to. I know more about the family trees of these criminals than I do about my own, and it's not because I wanted to." Gloria took a deep breath. Spots of red stained her cheeks, and her eyes flashed. "We fought that night about it, the night he—you know. He said some horrible things to me, then stormed out. He didn't come back to our room at the Bumblebee, and I tossed and turned all night. Not that the morning was much better."

Gloria turned to the side and pressed her fist to her mouth. Her eyes were still dry.

"It was that Greek man on the island," she blurted out. "The kiwi farmer. I know it. John dug too deeply, and he paid for it with his life. I hope the police lock him in jail and throw away the key."

Brianna murmured more condolences and backed away to give the woman space to grieve, although her gut told her that Gloria was performing the role of sorrowful widow more than feeling it. The most heartfelt part of her performance was her frustration over John's passion project.

Gloria's alibi might be sound—and she could check with Hilda, who owned the B and B—but it was possible to sneak out of a rented room without alerting others. Gloria wasn't off the suspect list, not at all. Her lack of sadness over her husband's passing, coupled with her hatred of his project, added up to a suspicious character. Unfortunately, Brianna didn't know of any plausible motive.

Gloria wandered to the tea table. Brianna studied the bulletin boards more closely. Pictures of John filled them, most of them professionally composed.

Someone sidled up next to Brianna and gazed at the

bulletin board. Brianna glanced at the wispy-haired man she'd noted earlier. He wore a polo shirt and jeans, although his bare feet were clad only in a pair of flip flops. Brianna shivered, thinking of the cold temperatures outside. Maybe he was channeling surfer vibes or was a proponent of the barefoot movement.

He met her gaze and nodded. "Such a tragedy," he said in a light voice. "To be taken from the world with so much more life to live."

Brianna murmured her agreement.

"How did you know John?" the man asked.

"I didn't, not really," Brianna admitted. "But I came to support my friend when she stumbled across the crime scene, and it felt right to pay my respects."

"Small towns can be very welcoming." The man smiled and held out his hand. "I'm Sam Brown."

"Brianna West." She shook his hand.

"I worked with John as his photographer. This whole fiasco was a shocker, no mistake." Sam sighed heavily. "His poor wife. John was a great guy—he didn't deserve this."

"You were fond of him?" It surprised Brianna to hear it. From her minimal interactions with the dead man, he'd appeared abrasive to everyone. Maybe he respected his colleague.

"Fond might be a strong term." Sam laughed lightly. "John was tough but fair. I had no problems with him. He wrote the articles, I took the pictures. It all worked out. The magazine will send a new journalist shortly to pick up where John left off, since we've already sunk resources into this article."

"Any idea of how he died?" Brianna glanced around to make sure Gloria wasn't in earshot. The other woman walked toward a back door, presumably to get some air and space from the wake attendees. "I saw the body, and it had been laid out like a ritual killing. Quite horrible."

Sam's mouth twisted. "I heard about that. I don't know who might have done it. Gloria is convinced that it's the Greek connection. I don't know, it seems farfetched. But John had been delving deep into that underworld. I suppose someone might have been unhappy with him unearthing secrets that should have remained buried."

"It would appear that way," Brianna agreed. "Gloria told me he left the bed-and-breakfast that evening after an argument and didn't return. You didn't see him leave, did you? See which way he walked?"

"Argument?" Sam shook his head and plucked a Nanaimo bar off the nearest platter. He took a bite of the layered square with a look of contentment. "No, I didn't hear that. I had to head back to Vancouver that evening. Family emergency. I was back on the island on the first ferry the next morning. Of course, John was dead by then."

Brianna's shoulders slumped. Sam tilted his head.

"What's your skin in this game?" he asked. "You seem to have a keen interest in John's death."

Brianna's cheeks warmed. She'd been too obvious, as usual. She should have dragged Macy here with her.

"They haven't found the killer yet," she invented. "I hate to think of someone like that walking around the streets of our little town, unchecked. I think we'll all sleep better at night once the person is behind bars."

Sam shivered and nodded. "Too true. I have to stick around until the police give us the all-clear, and finish my assignment for the magazine, but then I'm headed back to Vancouver. Who knew Snuggler's Cove would be the more dangerous place?"

He chuckled, and Brianna smiled politely. She hadn't learned much this visit, except that Gloria wasn't nearly as cut-up about her husband's death as she pretended to be and that she had no alibi.

"Like I said, Gloria's theory about the Greek crime families sounds preposterous but definitely worth exploring."

"Good advice." Brianna spotted the pregnant woman staring at the bulletin board with tears streaming down her face. She nodded toward her. "Do you know who that is?"

"Ah." Sam's lips thinned. "That's Krystal. John's estranged sister, or so she claims. She's the one who organized this wake."

"I should pay my respects." Brianna nodded at Sam. "Excuse me."

Brianna walked toward the bulletin board, intending to speak with Krystal. Before she reached her, the other woman released a sob and trotted heavily toward the bathroom.

Brianna sighed and took her plate to the hall's kitchen. Krystal was unavailable, and she'd given her condolences to Gloria. Her time would be better spent baking or maybe doing paperwork at home with Paprika on her lap.

She waved goodbye to a chattering Hilda and meandered to the entry hall, where she retrieved her coat from a hook. A chilly breeze whistled through the door when she opened it, and her shoulders hunched involuntarily to prepare for stepping outside.

Her bicycle leaned against the side of the community hall. She marched toward it, intent on biking home as quickly as possible to snuggle with Paprika in front of her propane fireplace.

Yelling stopped her cold. Brianna held her breath to listen. A woman shouted from behind the community hall. Patches of her irate voice carried on the wind.

"Worthless… should have been… now he's…"

Brianna crept closer and tucked inside a large rhododendron to spy. As she'd suspected, the strident voice emanated from Gloria Albright. But who was she shouting at? Was another person out there, or was she wearing an earpiece attached to her phone?

Brianna wrinkled her nose at the gusty wind interfering with her eavesdropping. How was she supposed to gather clues with it blowing all over the place?

Gloria shouted some more, but the wind tore her words away. A door slammed shut, and Gloria was mercifully silent once more, presumably alone now that her companion had gone inside.

Movement caught Brianna's attention. Devon Moore stood at the edge of the grassy clearing. He held a bouquet of lilies in one hand and wore a quizzical expression on his face.

"Gloria?" Brianna saw his mouth move with the

word, although she couldn't hear him.

Gloria's back faced Brianna, but she shouted loudly enough that Brianna caught occasional floating phrases.

"… just as bad…why are you… get out!"

Devon's mouth tightened. He looked like he wanted to say more. After a moment's consideration, during which he stared at the enraged woman, he turned on his heel and strode off. The flowers hung from his swinging arm.

Gloria's shoulders heaved with her panting breaths. For a long minute, she stared after Devon. Then she released a shriek to the sky, stamped her high-heeled boot, then marched through the back door of the community hall. The door slammed behind her.

Brianna stayed frozen in her bush for many long breaths to make sure the grassy area was empty. When nobody crossed her vision, she gingerly ventured out.

Mud sucked at her boot sole. She pulled it free, then whipped her head toward the place where Gloria had stood. She might not have seen whoever Gloria had been yelling at, but had they left any clues behind? Mud was an excellent canvas for tracks.

This altercation might have had nothing to do with John Albright's death, but Brianna wouldn't bet on that. Who was Gloria so enraged with that she would enter a screaming match in the yard behind her husband's wake?

Not that Brianna couldn't imagine Gloria screaming unprovoked. She appeared to be a volatile woman, unwilling to filter herself or maintain peace. She and John had probably suited each other, for unpleasantness if nothing else.

Brianna cautiously walked forward, glancing around until the entire area was visible. Nothing stood in the muddy grass surrounded by a semi-circle of maples except an old wooden bench with peeling turquoise paint that nestled against the back wall of the hall beside the closed door. A window overlooked the area, but its curtains were shut.

Brianna scanned the ground for clues. Gloria's boot prints were obvious, toes and spiky heels paired together. She must have had to balance on the balls of her feet to avoid sinking deep into the mud with her stilettos.

Devon's footprints walked a path from the opposite side, then retreated again. His large prints had a sturdy tread similar to Brianna's own, appropriate for the mucky winter weather.

The only other footprint visible wandered around the area and traced back into the community hall. Flat patches of medium-sized tracks had worn a spot in the mud a few paces away from Gloria's own. Brianna frowned at them. The footwear must have been so old that the tread had worn away. The person must have walked carefully to avoid slipping in the mud.

Someone had been out here with Gloria, unless a cleaning person had walked out before the wake. Brianna glanced around the mud one last time before retreating to her bicycle. She hadn't gleaned too much from this excursion. She would have to keep her nose to the ground for further clues.

Chapter 8

Brianna pedaled slowly back to the Golden Moon once she was sure no one else was outside watching her. The last thing she wanted was Gloria to know she'd been snooping.

A ray of sun pierced through heavy clouds from the horizon, bathing Brianna in a welcome beam of light before it set. It was almost closing time at the Golden Moon, and she wanted to start a few things for tomorrow before dinner. Paprika and her paperwork would have to wait for an hour or two. Oaklyn could probably use the company, too, and maybe some help with closing.

Brianna wheeled past the café's brightly lit and welcoming windows. Only two groups of customers sat inside, but Oaklyn was with another girl her age at the counter. Brianna narrowed her eyes at the dirty dishes on a table near the window. Was Oaklyn chatting with a friend instead of doing her job? Maybe she wasn't ready to be left alone yet.

Brianna parked her bicycle in the alley, locked it to the drainpipe, and entered the kitchen via its side door. She left her coat and purse on her desk, washed her hands, then entered the dining room, ready to confront Oaklyn.

Instead, Oaklyn's tear-streaked face greeted her.

"What's wrong?" Brianna asked, concern overriding her annoyance. Oaklyn's friend wasn't crying, but she looked grim.

"Our badminton team was going to go to the provincial championships." Oaklyn gulped. "But now we can't because Costas isn't allowed off the island because of this stupid investigation. I know it's dumb—it's only sports—but I really thought we had a chance this year."

"We totally did," her friend agreed. "A good chance to win, or at least place in our division. And now we'll have to wait until next year. Who knows what the team will be like then? Taylor and Quinn are graduating this year, so they'll be gone."

Oaklyn sniffled, and her lip trembled. "It's too much," she burst out. "On top of everything else."

Brianna opened her arms, and Oaklyn leaned into her. Brianna rubbed her back consolingly until Oaklyn straightened.

"It's rough all around," Brianna agreed. "Look, why don't you go to the back and run a load through the dishwasher, then clean yourself up a bit. Your shift will be over soon."

That was Brianna's attempt at balancing sympathy with reminding Oaklyn of her work duties. Oaklyn nodded and sniffed again.

"I should go," her friend said. She turned, then gasped. "Oaklyn, Riley's here."

"What?" Oaklyn dithered like a rabbit in front of a car. "What do I do?"

She quivered, then dashed into the kitchen. Brianna raised an eyebrow at the friend, who shrugged.

"He's hot," she whispered. "And Oaklyn likes him. He can't see her with mascara dripping down her face."

The friend gave a wise nod, then wandered toward the

front door, where the infamous Riley stood with someone who looked like his mother. The friend slipped by the other two, who approached the counter.

Brianna served them, one ear open for noises from the kitchen. When she heard the dishwasher starting up, her shoulders relaxed. Oaklyn had taken her hint. Now, Brianna wouldn't have to take a harder line, which she appreciated.

Once Riley and his mother had taken their loaf of bread and a bag of cheese scones and left, Brianna took the dirty dishes from the front table and headed into the kitchen. Oaklyn stood in front of the industrial dishwasher, waiting for the cycle to finish. More dishes waited to enter the machine.

"There's a lot to do, isn't there?" Brianna said.

"Yeah." Oaklyn glanced her way, makeup reapplied over her reddened eyes. "Sorry I didn't get to bussing that table."

"I'm wondering if I need to hire someone else." Brianna chewed her bottom lip. Another salary would take a chunk out of her profits, but the café was doing better and better each month. It was growing fast enough that a single employee grew overwhelmed if Brianna wasn't around to take up the slack. It might be time to put up a help wanted ad. Brianna much preferred baking to bussing tables herself, and getting someone else on the team would allow her more time to create new dishes. Like the pesky spanakopita she was working on.

"Something to think about," she said. "Anyway, I'm sorry to hear about your badminton tournament. That's rotten news."

"Yeah, well." Oaklyn shrugged, her don't-care façade back in place. She carefully didn't look at Brianna. "Whatever."

After a quick dinner in her float home that evening, Brianna returned to the café with trepidation. Christmas was fast approaching, and Magnus's summoning had held more than a little frenetic energy to it.

"You're here," Magnus exclaimed when she entered the glass door. "Good. Come in, don't dawdle. We have lots to get through today."

"We're decorating your cafe," Hilda explained when Brianna walked in with slow footsteps. Esme hadn't arrived yet, but Quentin stood primly in front of a stack of cardboard boxes, and Magnus glowered at them all.

"Right," he said. "Your café is woefully under-decorated. Snuggler's Cove has standards."

"And a contest," Quentin added. "For best decorated business. It's free advertising for a month in the island newspaper."

"That prize would be a boon to the Golden Moon." Hilda beamed at Brianna. "We can't let this opportunity slide by without at least attempting to take first place."

"As members of the Gourmand Society, it is our duty to help a fellow member represent the Christmas spirit," Magnus declared. "We have resources."

"I see that." Brianna peered with trepidation into the topmost cardboard box. A lot of tinsel garlands met her eyes. "Can we strive for tastefully understated?"

Hilda chuckled richly. "Oh, my dear, you are a hoot. With Christmas decorations, more is more."

With that ominous pronouncement, she pulled a large plastic reindeer out of the box and wandered toward the window ledge.

Esme walked in as Brianna rubbed her temple.

"Getting started without me?" she said to the room at large. "You'll need my expert aesthetic guidance. It can't just be throwing spaghetti at the walls. We need the decorations to flow together into a cohesive whole that simultaneously says, 'Christmas cheer' and elegance. Quentin, pass me that string of lights."

Brianna bit her lip at the colorful twinkle lights that emerged from the box, each light affixed with a dangling silver star.

"Why don't you fix us some tea," the older woman said when she noticed Brianna's pained expression. "Take your time. Don't worry, everything is under control."

"But whose control?" Brianna muttered. Esme's chuckle followed her as she fled into the kitchen.

Brianna spent far longer than she needed to preparing tea for all five of them and plating kiwi treats with garnishes of basil leaves. Finally, when she couldn't put it off anymore, she gritted her teeth, picked up the tray of tea things, and marched into the dining room.

The cafe was transformed. Brianna's jaw gaped open, and she gazed around the space. Tinsel garlands hung from every corner and draped in loopy swirls around the room. Every picture on the walls had decorations dangling from its corners. Quentin was hard at work with an aerosol can completing snow drifts piled on the windowpanes. Hilda directed Magnus as he stood on a café chair below a hanging light with a glittering mobile of holly and stars. Esme plugged in her last string of lights and sighed happily at the resultant rainbow glow. They'd pushed a few tables away from one corner to set up a towering artificial Christmas tree covered with ornaments.

After her initial shock, Brianna's heart pattered slower. It wasn't bad. She had braced for too much, and it was too much, but it somehow worked.

"You might have corralled 'more is more' into something beautiful," she admitted to Esme. "Congratulations."

"I told you not to worry." Esme cleared a table, and Brianna set her tray down. "With these decorations up, you have a fighting chance for that prize."

"Is that tea?" Hilda shuffled closer. Brianna handed her a steaming cup, and Hilda sank onto a chair to accept it. "And individual kiwi cheesecakes? If this is payment for decorating your café, my dear, then I gladly accept."

The five settled around the table, and Brianna handed out tea and treats. Magnus's salt and pepper hair glowed red from the lights strung on the wall. Tinkling music drifted from the windowsill. When Brianna raised an eyebrow at Quentin, he flushed.

"It's a motion-activated singing ornament," he admitted. "We can probably turn it off."

"Oh, Hilda." Brianna ignored the tinny music and turned to the elderly woman. "I wanted to ask you. Do you know the woman who organized John Albright's wake? Someone said her name was Krystal and that she's John's sister."

"Yes, Krystal Rivero." Hilda nodded and carefully placed her teacup on its saucer. "She moved to Driftwood Island a few years back. After that big storm. Do you remember, Magnus?"

"Yes," he said reflectively. "Three winters ago. It unmoored boats from the marina, and we lost power for a week."

"She has quite the belly on her these days." Esme leaned back in her chair and took a bite of her cheesecake. After swallowing, she said, "Don't know who the father is, though. Never seen a man around."

"I haven't heard who the father is, either." Hilda frowned, as if offended that there existed a piece of gossip that she didn't know. "She keeps herself to herself. Lives with that girl with the parrot, the one mooching off her grandparents. I heard she's a freelance editor and takes on jobs as they come."

"Good work for an island-bound person, editing." Quentin stirred sugar into his tea. "She can work remotely with no issue."

"An editor?" Brianna narrowed her eyes. "The photographer, Sam Brown, said something about her allegedly being John Albright's sister, as if he had doubts. Maybe she wasn't his sister after all but met him through work."

"You don't think…" Hilda leaned forward, her tea forgotten at the prospect of news. "Are you saying that the baby is John's?"

Brianna threw up her hands, horrified at how quickly

Hilda had jumped to conclusions from her musings out loud. "I'm not saying anything like that. She probably is John's sister. Why would Sam know anything about John's personal life? I just noted that they sort of work in the same general field."

Hilda leaned back, but her bright eyes gleamed. "It's a nasty business, this murder." She pulled a sock out of her purse and started to darn a hole with glittery gold yarn. "I can't believe they're still investigating, with no one in custody yet. The killer could be among us, and we wouldn't know."

Brianna willed herself not to look at the others. She'd suspected some of them of crimes in the past, and she didn't want to open old wounds. The Gourmand Society had proven itself again and again to be on the side of justice. She was done pointing fingers at any of them.

Unless she found them clutching a bloody knife over a body, of course.

"Tensions are high," Esme said. She languidly traced her finger over the tabletop. "I saw Gloria Albright in the Apple Cart parking lot with Corporal Devon Moore. I don't know what their history is, but she spat at him like some street hooligan. He, of course, didn't dignify her with a response and merely walked away."

"What an unpleasant woman," Quentin murmured.

"But why would she do that?" Hilda shuffled to the edge of her seat, her sock forgotten. Her eyes were bright with interest. "Do you think he cut her off in line and she's simply an ill-mannered woman? Or do they know each other?"

Brianna dithered on whether to tell the Society what

Devon had confided to her. Had he expected it to remain a secret? The knowledge hadn't seemed confidential.

"I think they were acquaintances," she said finally, keeping it vague. "Years ago."

"Oh!" Hilda blinked rapidly. Her hands trembled. Brianna expected it was from excitement rather than age. "Acquaintances. I'll have to find out more."

"Harrumph!" Magnus cleared his throat loudly. "That's enough gossip. How is everyone getting on with their Christmas dinner tasks? The event is less than two weeks away. Clearly, we have decorating in the bag—Brianna's café is testament to that—but what about the rest? Do we have a Santa yet?"

Brianna gaped at Magnus. With the murder of John Albright pushing everything else out of her mind, she hadn't given a single passing thought to her appointed task.

"Not yet," she said feebly. "I'll get right on it, though."

Chapter 9

The next morning found Brianna with her hands busy baking and her mind whirring with options for Santa candidates. She didn't know many people yet, that was the problem. The anniversary of her move to Driftwood Island wasn't for months yet. She flipped through customers in her mind's eye, but the one or two candidates who might work weren't regulars, and she didn't know how to contact them. She could call Dot, she supposed.

A person popped into her mind, and she stilled her hands at the mixer. Bacchus, the islander who considered himself the reincarnation of an ancient Roman god—and drank as much wine as he could muster to prove it—was the right build. Portly, older, and round-faced with a merry twinkle in his eye, Bacchus could easily wear a red suit with a cheery "ho ho ho" out of his mouth.

His merry twinkle and cherry cheeks frequently resulted from his adoration of wine, which gave Brianna pause. Yet, Bacchus always turned up for the annual autumn party he threw, so he was reliable. And if he wasn't, his partner Maenad was. She would get him to where he needed to be.

Bacchus would probably say yes. He was agreeable, and they were on speaking terms. Brianna nodded. Yes, she would approach Bacchus shortly and confirm his appearance as the wintery man in red.

Decided, Brianna finished her baking preparations and carried a fresh batch of scones to the counter in the dining room. Teri smiled at her but continued to serve her current customer. The dining room was almost full, with a five-person line-up. Mornings were often busy, with people wanting their coffee and pastries to start the day.

Brianna helped Teri make coffee orders and plate baked goods until the rush had calmed down. She took a moment to breathe, then Annalise from the neighboring yarn shop pushed into the café, pulling her sweater tighter around her substantial middle. Her gray hair piled in a loose bun on the top of her head, and her bubblegum pink glasses perched on the end of her button nose.

"My word, it's chilly out there today," she said in greeting.

"The perfect day to wear yarn creations." Brianna nodded at her neighbor's sweater, knitted in a medley of soothing greens and browns.

Annalise laughed richly. "Quite right. And also to have a warm drink. A mocha, please. With extra chocolate syrup."

"Coming right up." Brianna took a mug from the shelf and started preparing Annalise's drink. The other woman leaned against the counter.

"Have you encountered that new blond woman in town?" she said conversationally. "The loud one? She had a man with her a few days ago, but she seems to be on her own now. She came into the shop yesterday asking for—no, demanding—a piece of paper and a pen so she could write herself a note. I handed her my stack of sticky notes, and she proceeded to scrawl over three of them, then she stole my pen and left. Without buying anything, too." Annalise huffed a breath of disgust.

"That sounds like Gloria Albright," Brianna said, her hands busy with chocolate syrup. "She's a visitor in town. Her husband was murdered here, surely you heard the news."

"Oh, is that her?" Annalise's mouth opened with understanding. "Well, that changes things a bit. It's hard to act rationally when you're grieving."

"I'd like to say that's what happened, but I'm afraid she's always like that." Brianna topped the mocha with a dollop of whipped cream and handed the mug to Annalise. "Here, pass the mug back later, when you're done with it."

"You're the best." Annalise dropped a bill on the counter and bustled out of the café, back to her yarn shop. As she left, she held the door open for a heavily pregnant woman to enter the Golden Moon.

Krystal Rivero, the enigmatic so-called sister of John Albright, glanced at the rack of pastries under the glass-topped counter. Her tired eyes scanned the rows with nervous, flitting movements.

"They're all fresh today," Brianna said. "The Asiago jalapeño apricot scones are our bestsellers."

"I'll try one." Krystal spoke in a light, breathy voice. "And a decaf latte. I'm trying to be good for the baby."

Brianna placed a scone on a clean plate and prepared the latte. While it was steaming, she said to Krystal, "That was really nice, what you did for the celebration of life for John Albright. I heard you organized it all. He was lucky to have a caring sister like you in town."

"Yes, I was happy to do it." Krystal blinked rapidly. "Happy isn't the right word here, but holding the wake was the least I could do for my brother." She sighed and looked over the crowded dining room.

Brianna, seeing her opportunity to keep speaking with the other woman, came around the counter. "There's a free table over in the corner," she said, leading Krystal to a small two-person table next to the edge of the counter. "It's a busy morning."

Brianna pulled a chair out for Krystal, who settled heavily into it. Quickly, Brianna whisked a dirty dish off the table and grabbed the cleaning spray bottle and wiping cloth.

Krystal sipped her drink with a contented flutter of her eyelashes. "Oh, that's good."

"Do you think you'll be okay with the baby?" Brianna said, slowly wiping the table to prolong her stay. "It's not easy being a single mother."

"I hope so." Krystal tapped her fingers on her mug. "John promised to take care of me, but the last time we met, before—before he died, he was reneging on his promise. Said he couldn't afford to give me much for Gloria's sake." Krystal sat up straight with a glare in her eyes. "I don't think he gave two hoots about Gloria's feelings. I think Gloria found out he wanted to give me some money and was pressuring him to drop any connection to me."

"To his own sister?" Brianna said, her hand slowing on the table.

"I know." Krystal worried her bottom lip with her

teeth. "I mean, we weren't close, but still. Gloria held the purse strings in that relationship. I don't know, what if they had a fight over me and Gloria killed him? John was a very passionate man. I could see him standing up for his sister, insisting on giving me some money, and Gloria not accepting it."

"That's quite the accusation," Brianna said. She slipped into the remaining chair. Krystal didn't notice. She stared into her latte and swirled the contents.

"Funny how life goes," she said thoughtfully. "I had no idea that I'd end up a single mother, living with a roommate on Driftwood Island. It's bizarre."

"There are worse places to raise a child, from what I've seen," Brianna said. If Krystal had a roommate, Brianna might be able to confirm her alibi for the night of the murder. She would ask Macy to search for the roommate's name. Assuming Brianna could patch things up with her friend. "My friend Macy is a single mother of a teenager. She could probably be a sympathetic ear if you'd like."

"Thanks." Krystal took a resolute bite of her scone and chewed. The skin around her eyes crinkled in a smile. "I see why this is your bestseller."

Brianna watched Krystal eat and pondered this new information. Krystal's reasoning felt unsubstantiated. John might have stood up to his wife, but he also might have told his expectant sister that he wasn't planning to support her, which would make Krystal another suspect.

Still, she had heard too much circumstantial evidence against Gloria to ignore. She had nothing concrete to present to the detectives in charge of this case, but they needed to know everything she'd found to follow up with the best leads.

This afternoon, she would visit the Mountie detachment and tell them what she knew.

Brianna's palms were sweaty on the handle of the detachment's door. She took a deep breath.

"You'll be fine," she muttered to herself. "They'll want this information. And if they don't, then they're no further behind than they already were."

Her late husband had been a detective in Vancouver, but he'd always dismissed her interest in his work. Now, inadvertently, her brain painted all detectives with the same broad strokes, even though the previous two she'd spoken with had been nothing but kind and appreciative of her information.

Still, deep-set beliefs were hard to shake.

Brianna hitched on a pleasant expression and approached the front counter. "Hello," she said to Constable Lenox. "I have some information on the John Albright murder. Can I pass it on to the detectives involved?"

Lenox sat up straight. "You have evidence? A witness statement?"

"Nothing that concrete." Brianna tried not to let her heart sink when Lenox slumped back in his chair.

"You mean your gossip gathering." He sighed and stood. "Let me see if they want to talk to you."

Lenox disappeared down a corridor. Brianna leaned

against the counter and tapped her fingers in a frustrated staccato. Lenox didn't need to dismiss her information. Hadn't she been instrumental in the past, her and her "gossip gathering"? She missed Devon.

Lenox returned before she could grow too antsy. He waved at her to follow him.

"The case is cold enough that they're interested in anything you can provide," he said. "Just keep it short and to the point. They're very busy."

Busy with what, if they have no leads? Brianna wanted to say, but she held her tongue. She wanted the police force on her side, and being cheeky wouldn't earn her any favors.

Lenox opened the door to the break room and ushered her inside. It was plain, with a serviceable table in the center large enough to seat ten people. Only two sat at it. Brianna recognized the sandy-haired woman, but the hard-jawed man with her was new. His intense eyes stared at his laptop screen and only gave Brianna a cursory glance when she entered.

"Local bakery owner with potential information," Lenox told the two detectives seated at the table. "Name's Brianna West. This is Detective O'Sullivan and Detective Evron."

He backed out of the room and closed the door. Brianna swallowed her misgivings and tried to look competent and trustworthy.

"Please sit down, Ms. West," Detective O'Sullivan said with a nod. "Constable Lenox said you had information for us?"

"Cold, hard facts are best," said Detective Evron. He

shuffled papers in front of him. "Something we can use."

"I don't have any cold, hard facts." Brianna stiffened her spine and told herself to breathe. She focused on O'Sullivan. "But I have plenty of circumstantial information that might help guide your investigation."

Evron grunted but said nothing further. O'Sullivan gestured at her to continue.

Brianna laid out what she'd learned so far—Gloria dry-eyed at the wake and annoyed by John's passion project, the questions about Krystal and John's relationship—and was disheartened by the sneer on Evron's face that grew the longer she spoke. O'Sullivan asked a few follow-up questions.

"If that's everything," Evron said once O'Sullivan finished asking questions, "you're free to go."

Brianna stood, her fists clenched.

"And best stick to baking," Evron added. "We'll handle investigations from here."

Brianna's cheeks flushed hot. The arrogant man didn't even bother looking at her.

O'Sullivan stood and held out her hand. "Thanks for coming in." She threw a disgruntled glance at her colleague. "We appreciate you stepping forward with information."

"Just trying to help in whatever way I can." Brianna lifted her chin. "It's distressing to think about a killer on the loose in our sleepy little town. I want to see the person brought to justice as much as anyone."

Brianna left before her ire manifested in words she would regret. She marched down the corridor and outside into the breezy day. Clouds piled in the sky like frothy mounds of whipped cream. Brianna took a deep breath and released it.

"Come back soon, Devon," she whispered.

Since she was already out and about, Brianna rode to Bacchus's house to ask him about being Santa for the Gourmand Society's Christmas dinner. The ride cleared her mind and worked out the trembling from her limbs. She was angry at herself for reacting so strongly to Detective Evron's disdain. The fresh air blew away most of her frustrations.

By the time she pulled into Bacchus's driveway, her equanimity was restored. She flicked open her kickstand and walked past three enormous driftwood sculptures looming over the overgrown lawn. One might have been a standing woman, or possibly an abstract tower. It was hard to tell.

The house sank into the grass like it was tired, and its peeling brown paint didn't negate that impression. Maybe it was the weight of moss on the metal roof that pressed it downward. The scraggly grass was green in this season, but enough bare mud lay between plant patches that Brianna stepped carefully on the loose stone slab path that led to rickety stairs on the front porch.

She knocked firmly on the door. A full minute passed. She knocked again, then turned to walk away with her shoulders slumped. She had one job for the Gourmand Society's Christmas dinner. Would she come up short?

"Brianna West!" A jovial voice made Brianna spin

around.

A round man shorter than Brianna held open his arms in welcome. The grin above his stubbly chin was wide and infectious. His usual toga attire was complemented by a pair of stretched-out gray sweatpants underneath. Even reincarnated Roman gods must get cold in December.

"Bacchus," she said with gratitude. "You're home."

"What a lovely surprise! Oh, my donkeys just had a foal. You must come and look."

He bounded out the door and dragged Brianna down the steps by her arm. Brianna followed the exuberant man around the corner of the house. When the donkeys saw Bacchus, they hee-hawed loudly and trotted up to the fence.

"Look." Bacchus pointed proudly. "Isn't he cute?"

Brianna's breath drew in, and she huffed a laugh of delight. The little animal had perky, black fringed ears, with white around the deep black of his huge eyes. A sweet tuft of fluffy hair on his head made Brianna ache to pat it. The mother donkey gave her foal a nudge on the flank, and the little animal jumped sideways with a frisky kick of his legs.

"Incredibly cute," she agreed. "The sweetest little guy. Does he have a name?"

"Silenus," Bacchus said proudly. "We call him Silly for short, because, well, look at him."

"Silly works well." Brianna reached out a hand for the foal to sniff, but he shied away. The mother nuzzled her hand instead, and Brianna patted her head as a consolation prize.

"Speaking of children," she said in the most roundabout segue ever. "The Gourmand Society is putting on a Christmas dinner the Saturday after next. It's tradition to have Santa make an appearance to hand out presents for the children who attend. I was hoping you'd consider being our Santa this year."

"Me?" Bacchus's eyes were wide and childlike in his surprise. "You want me to be Santa? It's the belly, isn't it?"

He released a guffaw of laughter. It even hinted at a "ho ho ho", and Brianna grinned.

"It doesn't hurt the image, no."

"Of course I'll do it!" Bacchus threw his hands out as if to embrace the whole world. "I'd be honored. Just tell me the day, and I'll be there!"

Brianna left a few minutes later, after a last pat of the donkey, relieved and satisfied. She might not contribute much to the murder investigation, and her spanakopita was a joke, but at least she wouldn't let the Society down. Santa would arrive, as promised.

Chapter 10

The decorations at the Golden Moon made Brianna's eye twitch when she entered the space upon returning from her Bacchus errand. There were just so many strands of tinsel, strings of twinkle lights, and plastic figurines. She couldn't decide whether to cringe or to walk in proudly and own the overblown décor. But she couldn't deny it worked, in its own hyperbolic way.

"I think I'm going to go blind," Oaklyn muttered to Brianna behind the counter when she joined the girl there. She gave Brianna a faintly nauseated expression out of sight of customers. "It's a lot."

"I know." Brianna glanced around and sighed, although she was happy that Oaklyn was speaking to her again. Maybe she'd forgiven Brianna for her part in Costas's suspect status. "The Gourmand Society was trying to be helpful. I suppose it's festive."

Oaklyn raised an eyebrow over one thickly lined eye. Her usual aesthetic of black on black was the antithesis of the café this season. Brianna chuckled.

"A few more weeks, and it will be gone. Grit your teeth and get through it."

Oaklyn sighed heavily, then turned to an approaching customer with an attempt at a smile. Brianna left her to it and entered the kitchen to wash her hands. Her next batch of spanakopita wouldn't test itself. Happily, the kitchen was decoration free, so she could bake without the distraction of tinsel. If she needed a festive boost, she could poke her head into the dining room and get her fill.

She added hints of cinnamon, cloves, and allspice to her next batch of spanakopita for a mild seasonal kick. If she couldn't match the glory of the bought pastry, maybe she could create her own spin. It certainly smelled good coming out of the oven, and she waited impatiently for the triangles of individual phyllo servings to cool.

When she deemed them cool enough to not burn her mouth outright, she ate one over the sink to allow flakes of pastry to fall somewhere contained. It wasn't half bad, Brianna thought to herself. Nothing like that one she'd bought in Vancouver, but tasty enough to serve in the café. She grabbed a card from a shelf in her office nook and carefully wrote a label for the pastries.

Hilda Button's distinctive voice drifted through the open door between the dining room and kitchen. Brianna transferred the pastries to a tray and entered the main room.

"Hilda, how are you?" she asked the older woman. She placed the tray in the glass-topped counter and propped up the card she'd written. "Staying warm, I hope?"

"I do my best." She shivered dramatically. "That icy wind gets in your bones. What did you bring out? If it's hot, I'll try it."

"Seasonal spanakopita," Brianna said. "I'm testing recipes. Be my guinea pig."

"Don't mind if I do." Hilda pulled out her wallet and passed over some cash. With a wave, Brianna told Hilda to sit down. She grabbed the pastry plate and tea and took it to Hilda's table, where she was settling herself. The older woman arranged her coat on the back of her chair with fussy motions until it was just right.

"It looks splendid in here," Hilda declared to Brianna. "Simply splendid. The judges of the best decorated business always announce the winner at our Christmas dinner, you know. I'll be cheering for you."

"It was your doing," Brianna protested. "You and the Society need the credit."

"Don't be silly." Hilda flapped her hand at Brianna. "It's your café. And it looks splendid. Doesn't it, Pam?" Hilda leaned sideways and addressed another woman chatting with her friend at an adjacent table.

Pam looked startled but glanced around the café with fresh eyes. "The decorations? Very festive. Really gets me in the Christmas spirit. Is the Bumblebee putting on its Boxing Day tea this year? I love coming around for that."

"Of course." Hilda looked pleased. "Rosy includes my famous butter tart recipe every year." She turned back to Brianna. "It's a winner, that one. And see? Everyone loves the decorations."

Brianna wasn't sure Hilda's sample size of one counted as "everyone," but she appreciated the thought.

"Now, my dear." Hilda fixed her with a serious gaze. "Our young Corporal Devon Moore—I saw him in the hardware store this morning. He's looking very peaky. Positively mopey. This John Albright business, and him not going into work, must be weighing on him."

"I'm sorry to hear that." Brianna leaned against a chair

back and bit her lip. Something was going on with Devon. He had more history with the murder victim than he was letting on. What was causing him the most grief?

"He could use a friendly face." Hilda gave her a pointed look. "His place is on Kettle Lake, just past the Fireweed Road turnoff. It's a log cabin. You can't miss it."

"You want me to visit him?" Brianna blinked. "We're acquaintances, but I've never dropped by his place."

"There's a first time for everything." Hilda poured her tea and stirred sugar into it. "The best way to get to know someone better is to take a step forward. Trust me, he'll be glad of the company. Rattling around in that cabin by himself with nothing to do—he must be going round the bend."

Macy burst into the café the next morning.

"Brianna," she hissed at the door of the kitchen. Brianna whirled around from her mixer. Macy clung to the doorframe as if it were the only thing holding her up. Her eyes were wide, and her breath came in short bursts.

"What's the matter?" Brianna turned off her mixer and strode toward her friend. "You look like you saw a ghost."

"Not that far off." Macy took a deep, shuddering breath in. "You'll never guess. Hilda came into the preschool this morning to drop off her granddaughter, but she had news. Her daughter Rosy was delivering breakfast to the suites that ordered it, and she found Gloria Albright dead in her room. She found an empty bottle of sleeping pills next to her. They think she might have killed herself." Macy bit her lip hard. "The suicide note scrawled in lipstick on the mirror kind of gave that impression, too."

Brianna stared at her friend. "I can't believe it."

"I know, I wouldn't have guessed, either." Macy shook her head sorrowfully. "But she'd just lost her husband. That would depress anyone. Someone should have been with her. Did she not have any family or friends to help her through? I feel terrible. Maybe I should have reached out."

"That's a lovely thought, but I honestly don't think she was the sort to appreciate it." Brianna put a hand on Macy's shoulder. "But even if she would have, it's too late for regrets. I can't believe she killed herself."

"I know, it's hard to process."

"No, I actually don't believe it." Brianna narrowed her eyes and crossed her arms. "Gloria was a devout Catholic, according to Devon. Taking your own life is definitely against her religion. That doesn't mean she wouldn't do it anyway, if she felt driven to it, but there are other factors at play. Her husband had recently been murdered. Who's to say her death wasn't also murder but arranged to appear a suicide?"

"But why would the killer target Gloria?" Macy's brow creased. "I get the Greek crime family connection for John, but as far as I understand, Gloria didn't have much to do with the research."

"I don't know." Brianna tapped her fingers on her

arm, lost in thought. "But we need to find out."

"By the way, I'm sorry I was mad the other day," Macy said. "About you investigating Costas. I know it's the right thing to do, even though it hurts to consider him a suspect. Do you forgive me?"

"Of course," Brianna assured her, happy to be speaking with her friend again. "I understand."

Macy pushed herself upright from the Golden Moon's kitchen doorway where she'd been leaning. "I'd better get back to work. I'm only here because we have a few kids home sick, and I offered to do a coffee run for the staff."

"We'll talk later," Brianna promised. She returned to her cheese bread dough when Macy disappeared into the dining room, but her mind whirled. She spared a moment of sorrow and pity for Gloria Albright—however she'd died, and whatever her personality, she'd been taken before her time—but then thoughts of her investigation crowded to the forefront.

Had Gloria committed suicide? It felt so unlikely to Brianna, especially given her husband's murder. Gloria's death was too neatly done, too soon after the event. But why would the killer want her gone? And, if it was the same person, why hadn't they completed the same ritual as with John's body?

Brianna punched down her dough with vigor. Maybe that meant Driftwood Island wasn't hosting a random killer, which was a relief. Still, two deaths this week wasn't something to overlook.

"Brianna?" Teri popped her head into the kitchen. Her quizzical face glanced at Brianna's floury hands. "Do you have a minute? Someone wants a word."

"Tell them I'll be there in two minutes."

Teri disappeared. Brianna divided her dough into loaf-sized pieces, rolled them into the correct shape, and laid them in prepared pans. Then, she covered them with a cloth and washed her hands.

The dining room was half-full when she entered. Clinking cutlery and low chatter permeated the space, and Brianna's shoulders relaxed at the happy sounds. Teri nodded at a man and woman standing at the end of the counter. Brianna recognized the photographer Sam Brown from John Albright's wake.

"Hello," she said, approaching the two. "I'm Brianna West. I heard you wanted to speak to me. How can I help you?"

"I'm Yasmin Nouri." The woman held out her hand. Straight black brows framed large eyes above high cheekbones. Her full mouth opened in a friendly smile. "I'm a journalist with *Flights of Fancy*, a travel magazine. And this is Sam Brown, photographer for the magazine. We're here to do an in-depth article on Driftwood Island."

"We've met before." Sam smiled at Brianna. "Under sadder circumstances. Brianna was at John's wake, here on the island."

"I take it you're John Albright's replacement," Brianna said to Yasmin. "The magazine didn't waste any time."

"It's a little crass, isn't it?" Yasmin wrinkled her nose. "But the magazine schedules articles months in advance, and this travel piece is due to come out in the March edition. Since Sam was already here, my editor sent me along to finish what John had started. With that in mind, do you have a few minutes to answer some questions? I understand you're a recent arrival on the island, and I'd love to see the island through your eyes."

"I have a few minutes," Brianna agreed. She glanced at the timer in her hand. The bread would be a while yet, and she had fifteen minutes before her carrot cake muffins came out of the oven.

The others declined refreshments, so she ushered them to an available table. Yasmin hung her coat and purse off the back of her chair and pulled out a voice recorder.

"Do you mind if I record our chat?" she said. "I find the conversation flows much more naturally than if I take notes, and then I can quote you without error."

"I guess so." Brianna eyed the little device on the table between them. She placed her timer next to it so the recorder wouldn't look so intimidating by itself.

"Just ignore it," Yasmin said kindly. "Sam, why don't you grab some pictures while I speak to Brianna."

Sam nodded and stepped away, his summer footwear flapping across the floor. Teri looked askance when he aimed his camera at the display case, but with a few words of encouragement, she hitched on a smile and posed with a loaf of bread.

Yasmin touched a button on her voice recorder, then settled more comfortably in her chair. "Brianna, you opened your bakery-café this year, is that right?"

"In June," Brianna confirmed. She tried not to glance at the recorder.

"Wonderful. And how is it doing so far?"

Little by little, Brianna relaxed. Yasmin's manner was friendly and welcoming, a far cry from John's abrasiveness, and Brianna opened up about many aspects of business and island life. Yasmin was a good listener and asked just the right questions to further their conversation.

But as comfortable as their exchange was, Brianna hadn't forgotten her own goal. John Albright's killer was still on the loose, and Yasmin was someone else who had known the dead man. Maybe Brianna could glean some information about him from his former colleague.

At a natural lull in the conversation, Brianna jumped in. "I'm sorry about your colleague, John," she said. "It must have been a shock to the magazine. Did you know him well?"

"He was a valuable member of the team," Yasmin said, skirting the question. "A writer of great articles."

"He was difficult to work with, I imagine," Brianna guessed. Yasmin's glance downward confirmed it.

"We all have our foibles," Yasmin said delicately. "But his death was a tragedy, indeed. Silver lining, Sam can now move to another position. He's a skilled photographer, award-winning, you know. I don't know how, but John always had first dibs on Sam for his assignments. Sam is such a kind man. He must have been too loyal to John for his own good, even after all the flack John gave him. At least now he'll spread his wings."

Brianna blinked. Sam had seemed loyal, without rancor toward John. He and John must have had an understanding that Yasmin didn't know about.

"Did you know about John's passion project?" she asked the journalist.

Yasmin rolled her eyes. "You mean his crime family saga? Hard not to. It was a running joke not to be trapped in the elevator with John, lest he corner you with his newest theories and facts."

"Because of it, the police think a local man of Greek heritage might be behind John's death."

"Wait, is it—" Yasmin opened her phone and checked a calendar app. "Costas Dimitriou? We're interviewing him Thursday afternoon at his kiwi farm."

"That's the guy. I honestly don't think he's the killer, but if you have any information about John's project that might help me shed light on his death, I'd be grateful."

"And why you?" Yasmin tilted her head. "Why not the police?"

"They're doing a great job," Brianna assured her. "But they don't have ears on the ground like I do. When I can, I like to help them connect the dots."

"I wish I could help." Yasmin reached out and turned off her voice recorder. "I tuned out whenever John started yammering about his book. But given the way he died, and how far he stuck his nose into the crime world, it wouldn't surprise me if his prodding had caught up with him."

Chapter 11

Macy called Brianna as she was shutting down her kitchen for the afternoon. "Any news about the investigation? What have you found out so far?"

"Gloria Albright is definitely still a suspect in John's death, even though she's dead," Brianna said, happy to name someone other than Costas. "Crocodile tears at John's wake. And she was screaming at someone in the back—not sure who—completely ballistic. She was angry about something, and volatile enough to do something about it. She could have killed John then committed suicide from the guilt. Oh, and Krystal Rivero says she's John's sister, but there seems to be some doubt about that fact. I'm not sure what their connection is."

"Sounds like you've been getting around. Hey, are you free in about half an hour? I realized that it's already December fourth and I haven't done my Christmas shopping yet. I can pick you up?"

Half an hour later, Brianna said goodbye to Oaklyn at the front counter and wandered outside. She waited on the sidewalk under the Golden Moon's yellow awning to avoid a persistent drizzle. Macy's little red hatchback pulled to the curb a minute later. With relief, Brianna yanked open the door and climbed into the toasty interior.

"What do you need to get?" Brianna asked.

Macy groaned. "Everything! A little something for my

parents and grandmother, but mainly for Oaklyn. I haven't even started thinking about gifts yet. Do you have any ideas? Where should we go first?"

"What about some fancy soaps from that shop on Marigold Street?" Brianna suggested. She was at a loss about what a sixteen-year-old girl might want—it had been many years since Brianna had been one—but scented products were tried and true for a reason.

"Good call." Macy flicked her turn signal and careened around a corner. "Some more makeup from the pharmacy, too. Oh, and tape for her badminton racquet. I can't afford a new one, and the handle is falling apart. What else, I don't know. I'll take a trip to Vancouver next weekend if I can think of something to get her there. She'd love a phone, of course, but she'll have to save up for that herself."

"She has a job now," Brianna agreed. "Oh, she's talking to me again. A little, at least. Did you say something to her?"

"Yeah, we had a talk last night." Macy pressed the accelerator. "She's still emotional about the whole thing, but we gained some perspective. She recognizes that you're not trying to attack Costas, just find out the truth."

"Thanks." Brianna leaned her head against the headrest. "It's true. I want Costas to be innocent, too. But I want justice more."

"I get it." Macy sighed heavily. "I want to help. As fun as it would be to bury my head in the sand and ignore the facts, it's better in the long run to know the truth. So I did some digging into Krystal Rivero before I picked you up."

Brianna turned to look at her friend. "What did you find out?"

"Let's stop here first." Macy pulled into the parking lot of a small strip of shops. A pharmacy anchored the row, which also housed a bookstore and a children's clothing shop. "I'll get Oaklyn's makeup while we're here."

Brianna allowed Macy to park, but when her friend didn't resume their conversation by the time they exited the car and hustled under the shop's awning, Brianna threw Macy an impatient look.

"What did you find out?" she repeated. She glanced around to make sure no one was within earshot. "About Krystal?"

"Right." Macy glanced around as well. "Krystal Rivero isn't John Albright's sister. I found her actual family alive and well on social media. But what I also found was an online forum chat between Krystal and John from a few years ago. He was asking her about her editing work, then the chat got much chattier, if you get my drift."

"I knew she was lying." Brianna wrinkled her nose. "Do you think John is the father of her baby? How involved is Krystal in all this?"

"Hard to say. But with the innuendos being passed around—seriously, take it off a public forum—they certainly had the start of something. And if she wasn't his sister, why throw that celebration of life for him? My money is on a different connection than she's willing to admit."

"That's big." Brianna tapped her fingers on her thigh

absentmindedly. "I need to talk to her, see what she knows. Is she a suspect? But I don't know where to find her."

"And that's why I'm here. Krystal lives on Arbutus Drive, just off Windy Way." Macy crossed her arms and looked expectantly at Brianna. "You can say it. I'm a genius."

"You're a genius." Brianna gave her a swift hug. "Now I can visit her."

"What will you use as an excuse?" Macy frowned. "She might not want to spill the beans if you just turn up unannounced."

Brianna glanced around for inspiration. Her eyes fell on the children's clothing shop.

"I'll buy her some baby stuff," she said with a nod of satisfaction. "Say I felt moved to help after speaking with her at the café. Come on, you know about babies. Help me choose something for her."

"It's been a long time since I dealt with a baby," Macy said, but she moved toward the shop. "Have you seen how big Oaklyn is?"

"You have more experience than me." Brianna linked her arm with Macy's. "Help a girl out, here."

Brianna got out of Macy's hatchback and pulled her zipper up higher. The damp wind was bitterly cold and snuck into her jacket at every gap it could.

"Brr," Macy said, joining her. They looked at the bungalow before them. It was a small house, hardly more than a cabin, with an odd double roof like a pagoda. Cedar shakes covered what small expanse of outer walls wasn't interrupted by windows. A wraparound balcony invited them closer, but a green parrot in the window peered balefully at them and squawked loud enough to hear through the glass. A white wicker loveseat sat beside the door, growing moss in its crevices.

"This is the place?" Brianna stepped gingerly up a gravel path toward the door that was lined with a row of river rocks, each stone smooth and globular. Trim groundcover ringed the house, clearly cared for by the occupants. Was Krystal a gardener? Brianna knew nothing about her, besides that she was an editor and was pregnant.

And, she had a connection to John Albright.

Brianna knocked on the frosted glass of the door's inset window and waited. Macy shivered behind her and tucked her hands under her arms.

Footsteps approached, and the door swung open. A young woman stood on the threshold and stared at them through perfectly round glasses in a vibrant shade of peacock blue. Thick, dyed blonde bangs brushed the tops of the glasses, and the rest of her hair ended in a severe bob below her chin. A smear of green paint marred her cheek. "Hello?"

"Hi." Brianna gave an awkward little wave. "I'm Brianna, and this is Macy."

"I'm Darla. I'm not buying anything today, just so you know."

"No, we're not selling anything. We're here to say hello to Krystal. Is she in?"

"Yeah, she's here." Darla half-turned and raised her voice. "Krystal, visitors for you." She turned back and ushered them inside. "Krystal will be out when she's finished editing her page, no doubt. She gets really into her work. Come in, quick. I don't want Percival to get cold."

Brianna hopped through the door, but she raised an eyebrow. "Who's Percival?"

A loud squawk answered her question. Darla rushed to the green parrot's perch and cooed at the bird. "I'm sorry, doll. That was cold, wasn't it? The door is closed now, don't you worry your pretty little feathers about it. The room will warm up again in no time."

Brianna unzipped her coat in the uncomfortably hot, almost humid room. Large houseplants stood in corners and hung from hooks in the ceiling until the whole place looked like the jungle was taking over the floral-patterned couches and a wicker chair dangling from the roof. Brianna and Macy glanced at each other expressively.

"That's a beautiful bird," Macy said politely. "What type is he?"

"Percival is a male eclectus parrot," Darla said proudly, stroking the bird's head. He nipped her with his bright orange beak. "Ouch, Percy. Watch out for my fingie-wingies."

"He's lovely," Brianna said politely. "Is this your place? It's a wonderful spot in the trees."

Brianna was interested to know how this young woman could afford a house on her own, and Darla confirmed Hilda's gossip.

"It's my grandparents' cabin." She made a vague waving gesture around the room. "But they don't use it anymore, so they said I could stay here. And renting out the room to Krystal gives me spending money. It's a sweet deal. Now I can work on my painting career in peace and surrounded by nature."

"Is Krystal a good roommate?" Macy asked since the woman in question still hadn't arrived. "I mean, if you're looking for peace and quiet, sometimes having a roommate is hard."

"Too much alone time isn't good for the artistic soul, either." Darla adjusted her glasses and rubbed the paint smear on her cheek to little effect. "She and Percival keep me company. Although Krystal has become even more of a homebody since she got pregnant. Honestly, she's hardly left the house for the past two weeks."

"No evening engagements?" Macy said lightly, but Brianna knew where she was going with her questions. Could Darla confirm Krystal's alibi?

"Ha, no." Darla pursed her lips. "She just goes to bed and that's it. You'd think she'd want to take advantage of her last days of freedom before the baby arrives."

"Growing a human is hard work," Macy said mildly. "It's understandable."

She shot a look at Brianna, who nodded back slightly. Krystal was likely at home during John Albright's murder. Darla's assurances didn't mean that Krystal couldn't have snuck out after her roommate had fallen asleep, but her involvement in the murder was looking less likely.

Krystal wandered into the living room, rubbing her

eyes. She wore a baggy tee shirt over her round stomach with purple leggings poking out from the bottom.

"Hello," she said to the others in surprise, then squinted at Brianna. "I was just in the middle of editing. Thanks for making me take a break. Wait, you're from the Golden Moon café. Brianna, right?"

"That's right."

"Percival and I are going to watch a nature show in my bedroom," Darla announced. She held her arm in front of Percival's talons. The bird carefully shifted onto her hand, his wings lifting slightly for balance. Before they left, Darla turned to Krystal. "Can I borrow that red lipstick you have? I'm heading out tonight, and it would go perfectly with my dress. It's the same shade, that tomato-red look."

"Sure, it's in the bathroom." Krystal gave a tired wave to her roommate. With a regal nod, Darla swept from the room to a hallway with three doors and entered one. The closing door cut off Percival's parting squawk.

Brianna glanced at Macy. Krystal owned a tube of red lipstick. Gloria's so-called suicide note had been scrawled on the mirror with red lipstick. The shade wasn't that uncommon, but was it another piece of evidence pointing to the pregnant woman as the killer? If not of John, then maybe of Gloria?

Krystal shuffled to one couch and dropped onto it with a sigh. "That's better. What are you doing here? I don't remember saying where I lived."

"It's a small town," Macy said vaguely. She smiled at the other woman. "My name is Macy. I'm just tagging along with Brianna. We were out Christmas shopping."

"And I thought of you." Brianna held out the shopping bag. "You said you were on your own, and I know babies come with a lot of expenses. I wanted to help a little."

Krystal frowned in confusion but took the bag. She peeked inside and her expression cleared.

"It's so cute!" She pulled out a white onesie with a pattern of yellow ducks, then a receiving blanket in the same fabric. A tiny hat matched the ensemble. "You're so sweet. You didn't have to do this."

"It's tough being a single mother," Macy said. "Ask me how I know."

"It takes a village to raise a child, right?" Brianna waved at the bag. "Just doing my part to make Snuggler's Cove your village."

Krystal blinked rapidly. Brianna's insides squirmed a little. What she'd said was true, but she had another motive as well. Hopefully, Krystal wouldn't mind.

"That's lovely." Krystal wiped her eyes and laughed. "I can't tell if it's the pregnancy hormones or if I'm really that touched. Thank you."

"I assume the father isn't being much help?" Macy said. "My daughter's father moved away as soon as he heard the news. We were both teenagers, though. It was rough. So, I get it."

Krystal bit her lip. "I suppose it doesn't matter now," she breathed. "Everyone needs to know the truth if I want any inheritance money. I wasn't John Albright's sister. This," she pointed to her rounded stomach, "is John's baby."

Macy gasped quietly, and Brianna blinked. So, her

mad supposition had been correct. Hilda would dance with excitement if she were here.

"I see," Brianna said carefully. "Is that why you arranged the wake? So you could give a proper send-off for the father of your child? That makes sense. But I'm surprised Gloria attended. Didn't she know the truth?"

"We were very discreet." Krystal sighed and leaned more comfortably into the armchair. "I had no intention of breaking up his marriage. He had his life and I had mine, and that was exactly what I wanted. Gloria pretended that I'm John's sister for appearance's sake, but I think she knew. Or at least was suspicious. That's why she came on this trip to Driftwood Island with John. She didn't normally travel with him, but this time she insisted. She must have figured it out."

"So, you're going to come forward now and try to get some inheritance money from John's estate." Macy glanced at Brianna, her incredulity clear. "I mean, I wish you the best, but I hope you have a good lawyer."

"I know, it's a long shot." Krystal seemed close to tears again. "I probably won't get anywhere with it. I'm so angry that John is dead. Sad, obviously, but at least if he were alive, I could beg him to reconsider his stance, or get the courts to force him to pay child support. It would be so much easier if he were still alive." She muffled a sob with the back of her hand. "And then my poor baby would have a father. I never wanted this."

Brianna exchanged another look with Macy. Krystal seemed less and less likely to be a suspect in John's death.

"And now it's my fault he's dead," Krystal wailed suddenly.

Brianna wiggled forward on her seat. Was this a confession?

"How do you mean?" she said.

"If I hadn't told John about the Greek kiwi farmer, he never would have come here to investigate." She drew in a shaky breath. "I'd chatted with Costas briefly at a summer barbecue. When I mentioned him to John—and that he was from Thebes, originally—John could hardly contain himself. I'm sure Costas killed him, or at least put a hit on him to protect his secrets. And I made the connection."

Tears streaked down Krystal's face, and she pulled out a tissue to wipe her cheeks. Brianna leaned back in her seat, disappointed. Not that she wanted Krystal to be the killer, but a confession would have exonerated Costas and completed her investigation tidily.

"I know John had some shady things in his past," Krystal continued. "But still, I told him about Costas. That's on me. And now he's dead."

She pressed her fist against her mouth with an anguished expression. Brianna's heart leaped. What did Krystal know about John?

"What kind of shady things?" Brianna said with as much delicacy in her tone as she could muster. "Poor man, surely nothing could be so bad as to deserve his fate. Life is cruel."

"It is," Krystal sobbed. "I don't know much, just that he moved out west years ago because of some trouble back there. Something on the wrong side of the law. I don't understand it. He was always good to me. Except for the support, but I blame Gloria for twisting him on that front."

Macy passed Krystal another tissue, and the younger woman blew her nose loudly.

"We should leave you in peace," Brianna said. "I'm sorry we disturbed you and brought about tears. That wasn't my intention."

"This is half my life at the moment." Krystal gave a watery chuckle. "If it's not grief at John's passing, it's hormones. Don't blame yourself. And thank you for the baby things. It was very sweet of you to think of me."

They said their goodbyes and left a red-eyed Krystal to get back to her editing work. Once they were safely ensconced in the car, Brianna turned to Macy. "She's not our killer," she said with regret. "She had too much to lose with John's death."

"And the belly on her." Macy turned the key in the ignition, and the car coughed to a start. "There's no way she was hauling a fully grown man into a ditch. Trust me, just hauling yourself around is awkward enough. And she's not a big woman."

"You're right." Brianna sighed. "And her roommate corroborated her alibi. Krystal isn't a suspect. Not for John's death, anyway. Maybe Gloria's."

"Ooo, there's a thought. Still not sure how the mama-to-be would win against Gloria, but maybe she poisoned her or something. But, setting that aside for the moment, who killed John?" Macy bit her lip and turned a corner. "And what's with this shady past of his? That's worth investigating."

"Whatever it was, it happened back east. Devon said he knew John back in Saskatchewan. Maybe he knows what this shady past is.”

“It looks like you have a handsome Mountie to question.” Macy laughed at Brianna’s exasperated glance. “I’m just saying, he’s a hottie.”

“I’ll talk to him, but it’s a tenuous association. Although he knew John. I’ll visit him at some point, for sure.”

“If it’s today, I can’t join you, which is probably for the better. He might be more open to discussing secrets with you by yourself. I need to get home and make dinner for Oaklyn. Where can I drop you off?”

“As close to the Bumblebee as you can get,” Brianna said. At Macy’s raised eyebrow, she clarified. “Hilda knows everything, and John and Gloria were staying at the B and B. I need to see what she knows.”

Chapter 12

Hilda had her hands in the dirt of a planter box that hung on the railing when Brianna arrived. Daylight was fast dissolving into the dark gray clouds, but Hilda hummed happily. She poked at the dirt with a trowel.

"Brianna, dear," the older woman said when she saw her approach. "How lovely to see you."

"What are you doing gardening at this hour?" Brianna said with a smile. "And in December?"

"Getting rid of the old chrysanthemums." Hilda pointed at a bucket of dead plants at her feet. "My son-in-law is bringing me some fir boughs from the forest tomorrow. I'll jazz up these empty planters, add some outdoor decorations. They'll be festive in no time." She dusted off her gloved hands. "And I was at loose ends after my early supper. Why not get out in the fresh air? The porch light is certainly bright enough."

"Why not, indeed. Can I help you take away that bucket?"

"No, don't you worry about it." Hilda peeled off her gloves. She placed her hands on the small of her back and stretched with a groan. "I'll get my son-in-law to deal with it tomorrow. Come in, come in. Would you like a cup of tea?"

"I should get home soon," Brianna said. "Get myself some dinner, feed my cat, Paprika. But I wondered if I could see one of your rooms."

"Having visitors soon?" Hilda perked up. "Your float home probably doesn't sleep many. The Bumblebee is a good idea for extra guests."

"No, nothing like that." Brianna made a mental note to invite her brother to the island sometime soon. "I was hoping to see the room John and Gloria Albright stayed in before he passed away. Unless Gloria was still in it when she died."

"No, we moved her to another suite." Hilda gave a sage nod. "The police were investigating, weren't they? And Rosy thought she'd be more comfortable in a room that didn't remind her of her late husband. Then she took her own life." Hilda clucked her tongue in sympathy. "Sleeping pills would be a peaceful way to go, I suppose. Not a surefire way to pass, though. Too likely to end up with brain damage, not death. But I don't know what she was doing with her wrists before then. Red and raw, they were."

Brianna raised her eyebrows. "Trying an alternate way to end things, maybe?"

"What, with a spoon? It's probably unrelated. Now, what were you hoping to find in the room?"

"Clues," Brianna said vaguely. Her mind turned over Hilda's revelation about Gloria's wrists. Had she been in an altercation before her death? Was this a clue pointing to murder instead of suicide? But that note in lipstick on the mirror pointed toward self-harm. "Something the police might have missed. I'm still trying to clear Costas Dimitriou's name. I'm hoping he's innocent, but I need proof."

"The police were thorough," Hilda said. She glanced

around, then leaned closer. In a stage whisper, she said, "But follow me."

Intrigued, Brianna followed Hilda through the Bumblebee's main entrance. The older woman shuffled past the dining room and down a carpeted hallway. When they turned a corner, Hilda entered one of the closed doorways.

"My suite," she explained. "It works out well. I get my own space, and Rosy has the cleaners take care of it. Come in. You're sure about that tea?"

"I'm sure."

Brianna followed Hilda inside her suite. It was bright and cheerful, with tall windows letting in streaming sunlight from a rare break in the clouds. Two comfortable armchairs faced each other with a coffee table between them, covered with an embroidered tablecloth in tiny flowers.

"My mother made that," Hilda explained when she caught the direction of Brianna's gaze. "I never had the patience for embroidery."

"It's lovely."

"It's sentimental." Hilda chuckled. "But that's me to a tee."

Brianna looked around the shelves and dressers filled with knickknacks and photos and concluded that Hilda knew herself well.

"Oh, before I forget," Brianna said. "I've been meaning to ask you about the suicide note Rosy found after Gloria's death. Do you remember what it said?"

"That's asking a lot out of this old noggin." Hilda chuckled. "But Rosy took a picture. I'll get her to send it to you if you're interested."

"Please." Brianna could have hugged Hilda. The busybody was invaluable to an amateur investigator.

"Now, I'm sure I put those papers somewhere safe." Hilda bustled around the room, eventually landing at a small rolltop desk in a corner. It was stuffed with bits of paper and pens and was one of the few untidy areas of the suite. Hilda caught Brianna glancing at it and chuckled. "I don't allow the cleaners near my desk. There's order to my chaos, and I won't have others prodding around my papers. Ah, here they are."

Hilda pulled out three crumpled sheets of paper from a small cubby. She smoothed them on the desktop, then brought them over to Brianna, who took them with interest.

"Rosy found them in the garbage from John and Gloria's room," Hilda explained. "She took them out because they ought to go in the recycling, you know. The detectives must have missed them. Luckily, I spotted them before Rosy took the recycling to the curb. I don't know if they're of use to you, but they're the only thing I could salvage. The writing is terrible, though. I haven't deciphered the words yet, not with my old eyes."

Brianna skimmed the pages, which were covered with spiky handwriting. Her brow contracted.

"It looks like a rough draft of John's manuscript," she breathed. "Yes, look at this. A sketch of a family tree, and a paragraph about some family called Michelakis. Wait, this part is talking about ritual killings. 'A unique practice of the Theban Michelakis family is the ritualization of their kills. If a person wrongs the family, they are not simply executed. They lay the body out in state in a prominent place with slices of feta cheese on the eyes. They do it secretly, at night, so the local constabulary can't pin the crime on a particular person. Of course, the police know—the Michelakis family specialize in feta cheese production, and this ritual is well known in Thebes—but an uneasy truce exists between the Michelakis family and the authorities. They mostly don't interfere with one another.

"'However, in recent years the Michelakis family has slowly and insidiously positioned key family members in all layers of government. This is not as well known, but through careful investigation, I have uncovered…'"

The rest of the sentence truncated with the end of the page.

Hilda's eyes were wide behind her glasses. "Ritual killings?" she whispered. "Didn't you say that John's body was laid out like that, cheese and all?"

"I did." Brianna scanned the rest of the sheets, but nothing else jumped out at her. Her mind whirled with this revelation. "If he was threatening to expose their role in corrupting the government in Greece, it explains how he irritated them enough to kill him."

"But Costas isn't a Michelakis," Hilda said with confidence. "His last name is Dimitriou. He's not part of this."

"Names can be changed," Brianna said absently. She scanned the pages again, then looked up. "Who knows what his mother's maiden name was, for example."

"It doesn't look good for Costas," Hilda said.

"No," Brianna agreed. Her heart sank as she thought

of Macy and Oaklyn, then of Costas's beaming face. Was he the killer? "It doesn't look good at all."

After a little more chatter with Hilda about the case, Brianna took her leave. When she passed the front counter of the bed-and-breakfast, a familiar voice stopped her steps.

Detective O'Sullivan spoke to Hilda's daughter Rosy. Rosy's round, cheerful face looked uncharacteristically solemn as she answered the detective's questions and nodded her head, her short brown curls bobbing with the motion. O'Sullivan jotted down notes on a pad as Rosy spoke.

Detective Evron stood behind O'Sullivan, his face wreathed in its usual glowers. When he spotted Brianna, he strode toward her. "What are you doing here?" he said gruffly.

Brianna frowned at him. "Why shouldn't I be here? I live in Snuggler's Cove and visit my friends around the island."

"I assumed you were here to snoop around for clues concerning the Albright case," he said.

He wasn't wrong, so Brianna remained silent. He must have taken her lack of answer for consent because he grimaced and shook his head.

"You need to stay out of it," he said. "Leave the investigation to those who are qualified to handle it."

Brianna bristled at his words. Hadn't she been helpful in the past? It wasn't like she was trampling around crimes scenes, destroying evidence. She was merely gathering information in ways that the detectives likely couldn't. The right gossip, told by the right people, could be a gold mine of knowledge.

"Did you see these?" Brianna pulled the papers Hilda had found out of her purse. They were crumpled and not as impressive looking as she'd hoped, but she presented them anyway. "Hilda Button found them in the trash of John Albright's room after he passed. They look like a rough draft of the book he was writing. There might be clues."

"I saw them." Evron waved at the papers dismissively without taking them. "They say nothing we don't already know."

Brianna's lips tightened at the stubborn detective before her. She shoved the papers back in her purse.

"And I hope you noticed the state of Gloria Albright's wrists," she said. "They were apparently very red and raw for someone who committed suicide via sleeping pill overdose. Maybe it wasn't suicide after all?"

"Stick to baking," Evron growled. "You'll only get yourself into trouble with your amateur investigations. And I don't want you interfering with police business and potentially messing things up."

He turned his back on her and strode to O'Sullivan. He then stood with his arms crossed and his eyebrows almost touching.

Brianna huffed and spun around to leave. She'd done what she could in the face of such an obtuse and stubborn detective. She would have to continue searching her own way, without alerting Evron. He was becoming an obstacle on her path to justice.

The next afternoon was cheese wheel day. The café was full of excited onlookers, and Oaklyn was busy ringing through orders and warming scones for the chattering crowd. Brianna helped her make coffee orders until the delivery van rolled up, then she strode to the front door.

"Corinne, hello," she greeted the van driver. She liked getting to know her fellow islanders.

"Hi, Brianna." Corinne checked her clipboard, then hauled open the back door of the van. "Looks like you've got your monthly cheese order here. Can you manage it?"

"I've got it," Brianna said with assurance, although she started second-guessing her blithe confidence when Corinne pulled a hefty bucket from the back, and it landed heavily on the sidewalk. Liquid sloshed inside the clear container, and a huge floating chunk of cheese pressed against the side.

"It's sealed tightly, by the looks of it." Corinne answered Brianna's unspoken question. "You should be able to roll it into the café."

Brianna stared at the tub, her heart sinking. She'd forgotten that she'd ordered feta for this month's cheese wheel day. In light of John Albright's murder situation, the choice felt crass. The only saving grace was that few people knew about the feta connection.

She gritted her teeth and pushed the container onto its side. Brine slopped around inside. She rolled it across the sidewalk and through the café door that a helpful patron held open for her.

The customers gave a cheer when the cheese entered the dining room. Brianna waved and rolled the bucket to the counter, where she gave a short spiel about feta's history and attributes. Then, she cracked open the container, sliced off a chunk, and cut it into small pieces. Oaklyn grabbed a tray and passed around the samples for patrons to try.

"It's tasty," Oaklyn said once she'd finished passing out pieces of cheese and was nibbling on her own in the kitchen. "I like its saltiness."

"And so creamy," Brianna agreed. "I can't wait to try this batch inside my spanakopita."

"What's with the spanakopita obsession lately?"

"I—" Brianna hesitated. She wanted to develop a recipe that would rival the product she'd eaten from Vancouver because if she couldn't claim the best pastries in British Columbia, could she really expect people to continue to buy from her café?

Her line of reasoning sounded silly when she thought of explaining it. Brianna wasn't in the mood for Oaklyn poking holes in her argument, so she said instead, "I want to make sure I get it right. People expect tasty things when they eat at the Golden Moon."

"Your stuff is good," Oaklyn said dismissively. "People are here, aren't they? You're worrying too much."

"Maybe so. It's hard not to worry when your livelihood depends on it, though."

Oaklyn gazed at her, thoughts clearly churning in her

mind. "Yeah, I get it," she said, and Brianna saw she did. With Macy as a single mother scraping by, Oaklyn had likely seen her fair share of money worries. "But look at it this way. Where are people going to eat and drink coffee? Hilltop Farm only sells their cinnamon buns on the weekends, and the Bumblebee is okay, but not as good as your food. Then you have that hipster coffee shop by the ferries, but seriously, no competition. People can get coffee and doughnuts at the chain restaurant out of town, but you don't want those kinds of people, anyway. So not worth trying to win that type over." Oaklyn spread out her hands as if to emphasize her irrefutable point.

Brianna chuckled. "The Golden Moon is the default less bad option, is what you're saying."

"No!" Oaklyn stamped her foot. "I'm saying that it's obvious why people like it here and that you have nothing to worry about. Honestly."

"I appreciate that." Brianna smiled at her young employee, who still wore a mulish expression. "I'll try to remember it. But I still want to make my baking the best it can be. No resting on my laurels, here. And it's personal, now. The spanakopita can't win."

"That, I can get behind." Oaklyn grabbed another piece of feta and popped it into her mouth. "I remember not liking this stuff when I was a kid. Only marble cheese for me. Things change, I guess."

"For the better." Brianna shook her head. "Marble. I mean, it has its place, but the wide world of cheese is so much greater than that." Since they were speaking again, she said, "About Costas—"

"Do we really need to go there?" Oaklyn crossed her arms with a defiant expression. "I'm trying not to think about the whole terrible situation."

"I only wanted to say how sorry I am about everything. I really hope he is innocent and that the detectives can find evidence for the actual killer soon. Costas seems like a great guy, and I don't want to think of him like that."

"Yeah, me neither." Oaklyn's lips tightened. "For my mother's sake, and for my badminton team. We have a chance to win the provincial championships if we go. It's a small chance, but still. I wanted us to try."

Impulsively, Brianna wrapped her arm around Oaklyn's shoulders and gave her a squeeze. The girl didn't pull away, which Brianna took as a good sign.

"I'm doing my best to help the detectives figure out the truth," she said. "I want to sort this out too. And if Costas isn't the culprit, then no one will celebrate louder than me."

Oaklyn gave a sniff, then stood straight. "Customer," she said with a nod to the dining room. "I'd better go."

She left the kitchen. Brianna rested her palms on the counter behind her. Costas was still a suspect, unfortunately, but at least Oaklyn didn't seem to hate her for it.

"Oh, Brianna." Corinne entered the café again with an envelope in her hand and poked her head into the kitchen. "With all the excitement over cheese wheel day, I forgot you had another delivery. Here you go."

"Thanks, Corinne." Brianna waved at her and tucked the envelope away on her desk in the kitchen. The café was still busy, and Oaklyn needed her help. She would examine the contents of the envelope when she had a moment to herself.

Brianna heaved a sigh of relief when the last patrons wandered out the café door. Bacchus wandered past her customers in front of the large windows, chuckling to himself as he weaved his way down the sidewalk. Brianna frowned. She hoped he would pull himself together for the Christmas potluck.

Oaklyn locked the door and flipped the open sign to closed.

"That was amazing," she said. "Who knew so many people wanted to taste a bit of feta cheese?"

"More than I expected," Brianna agreed. "If you want to bring the plates and cups into the kitchen, I'll deal with the dishwasher since I'm here."

Oaklyn visibly perked up, and she grabbed a tray to gather dishes. Brianna walked into the kitchen and sank onto her desk stool with a sigh. She'd get to work when Oaklyn appeared with the dishes. Until then, she would rest her weary feet.

Her phone pinged, and she slid it out of her pocket. As Hilda had promised, Rosy from the Bumblebee had texted a photo of Gloria's suicide note. Brianna eagerly opened the picture and peered at the image.

It was scrawled in tomato-red, spiky letters across the bathroom mirror. The words said, "I can't live without John. Pray for me."

Brianna blinked and shook her head mournfully. She had doubts about Gloria's suicide tendencies, but the note was poignant. Maybe she had been too distraught to consider her moral stance and had succumbed to her despair. And maybe their relationship had held more affection than they'd ever shown in public. Something about the note didn't sit right with Brianna, but she couldn't put her finger on what. She wished she had a sample of Gloria's handwriting to check if the woman had written the note herself.

She stared harder at the note. The lipstick was a bright, tomato-red shade. At the market when Brianna had glimpsed Gloria for the first time, as well as at the wake, the other woman had been wearing lipstick in a deeper, cherry red hue. Lipstick wearers tended to be creatures of habit. Brianna found it unlikely that Gloria would have switched shades of red.

Another lipstick user crossed her mind. Krystal owned a tube of tomato-red lipstick. The pregnant woman hadn't killed John Albright, Brianna was certain, but could she have murdered his wife? If Gloria stood in the way of the baby's inheritance, Krystal would have had motive.

She sighed and put the phone down, too tired to ponder the mystery of Gloria's death. The envelope that Corinne had delivered earlier caught her gaze. It was large, the size of a sheet of paper, and weighty. Brianna slit it open.

Large photographs spilled onto her lap. Brianna glanced at them, uncomprehending. Then her heart pattered faster.

Each photo was a picture of her. In them, she was riding her bike, serving customers at the Golden Moon, entering her float home, and walking with Dot on the sidewalk. Each photo had trees and lampposts framing the sides, as if taken from a distance.

Brianna's fingers tightened on the edges of the photos. She slammed them onto her desk and picked up the envelope. Except for her address, it was blank. She shook the envelope upside down, then sifted through the photos. No note appeared.

Her breath came faster. Someone was following her, and they wanted her to know it. Was it the killer, trying to dissuade her from investigating?

Her first thought was Sam Brown, the photographer, but she dismissed him immediately. He hadn't even been in town the night of John Albright's murder.

Costas popped into her mind. He'd admitted to her his love of bird photography. It wasn't a stretch to imagine him taking threatening photos of her with his camera.

Brianna shivered and wrapped her arms around herself. She wasn't that easily discouraged, but knowing that someone was watching her at all times was highly disconcerting. The murderer was cold-blooded enough to carefully arrange John Albright's dead body. Why would they hesitate to silence Brianna?

Oaklyn clattered into the kitchen with a full tray of dishes. Brianna jumped up, happy to have a distraction from her dark thoughts.

"Pop them on the counter," she directed. She smoothed her shaking hands over her apron. "I'll handle them."

Chapter 13

Oaklyn closed the Golden Moon's till with a clang.

"We're out of loonies," she said out loud. "We'll need some for tomorrow. Want me to go to the bank before they close?"

"Don't worry about it." Brianna sipped her tea, allowing the warm liquid to soothe her shattered nerves. "I'll go. You've worked hard today. Go on and have some fun."

Oaklyn's mouth twitched in an almost smile before she ripped off her apron and grabbed her black raincoat. Brianna waved her off, and the girl disappeared out the front door.

Brianna examined the till. Only a few one-dollar coins remained, as Oaklyn had said, but they were running low on quarters, too. She took her purse from a cubby beside her desk and slung it over her shoulder. Involuntarily, she glanced out the café windows. No one was outside watching her, but how far could a zoomed-in camera lens see? Costas's camera crept into her mind, and she shivered. Maybe he only used it for birdwatching, and maybe he didn't.

She was trying her best to be objective and look at all the facts—trying her hardest to find someone other than Costas as the killer if she was being honest with herself—but the circumstantial evidence was mounting up.

Brianna locked the Golden Moon behind her and

strode with swift steps toward the bank.

"Don't look around," she told herself sternly when fear prickled the back of her neck. "Don't give any watchers the satisfaction."

To distract her racing mind, Brianna cast her thoughts to the regulars who frequented the café. Corporal Devon Moore sprang to the forefront. She realized with a pang that it had been many days since he'd stopped in. Hilda had said he'd been looking mopey.

He must be bored, with no work to structure his days. She wondered if he had many friends on the island. He'd only arrived a few months before she had, after all. She'd been lucky knowing Macy and Dot already. Others on the island were welcoming, but friendships took time to mature.

Maybe she should go see him. It was the neighborly thing to do. He was probably yearning for a friendly face.

And then she could show him the photos and get his opinion on how concerned she should be. Brianna nodded and flung open the bank's glass door. Yes, she would do that. The photos would worry him, but she was too far into this murder investigation to back off now, and he would likely agree to that. And if he knew, he could give her advice on how to proceed.

After retrieving a few rolls of coins from a bored teller, Brianna walked through the chilly afternoon air in Snuggler's Cove. On her way down a road perpendicular to the bay, something shiny in a store window caught her eye.

It was an antique shop, one that Brianna had frequented in her first months on Driftwood Island when searching for old cheese knives and other décor for her café. Christmas decorations filled the window of the shop, but every single one was antique or vintage. A wooden rack glimmered with blown glass ornaments, colored tin twists hung in a row along the top of the window, and a sweet stuffed teddy bear sat in the corner with a Santa hat perched jauntily on its head.

Brianna blew air out of her mouth contemplatively. It was a splendid display. Incredible, in fact. The way it all matched with the shop's theme was brilliant, and everything glimmered and sparkled with holiday cheer. That was true festive spirit.

The gnawing of jealousy bit into Brianna's heart. The Golden Moon was decorated, extensively so, thanks to the Gourmand Society—but it wasn't as spectacular as this antique shop. If she was going to be a contender in this decoration competition, she wanted to do it properly.

She strode past the antique shop and turned into the pharmacy next door. Seasonal décor hung on racks beside the front door. Brianna frowned as she fingered through the sparse offerings.

"Is this everything you have for Christmas decorations?" she asked the woman behind the counter who wore a tie-dyed bandana over her frizzy brown hair.

"That's it," she said, with too much cheer for Brianna's liking, given her disappointing news. "Most people have already bought what they need."

Brianna grabbed another two rolls of tinsel and the last paper banner decorated with pictures of holly. "I'll take these," she said. "I didn't realize how late I was this year. Next year, I'll have to get on it earlier."

The woman chuckled and rang her purchases in. "We take the festive season seriously in Snuggler's Cove. You run the Golden Moon, right? Are you trying to win the competition?"

"I thought I'd throw my hat in the ring," Brianna said with feigned nonchalance. Her competitive side was itching to give it her best shot.

"You have your work cut out for you. Annalise's yarn shop and the salon are gorgeous this year. Annalise even has knitted snowmen hanging in the window. But the hardware store might just take the cake, with that huge handmade sleigh beside the front counter. Best of luck!"

Back at the Golden Moon, Brianna glanced at the neighboring shop. Just like the other shopkeeper had mentioned, Annalise's window was a testament to festivity. The knitted snowmen looked particularly fetching, and crocheted snowflakes made from a glittering white yarn surrounded them, held up by invisible fishing line. On an impulse, Brianna pushed the door open.

Soothing sounds of rainfall and tinkling harps drifted through the still air of the yarn shop. Fabric bins of colorful skeins clustered around the edges of the shop and lined the walls in honeycombs of soft color.

Brianna walked across the tiled floor toward the back counter, where Annalise's backside stuck up into the air as she rummaged for something.

"Oh! You startled me," she said with a laugh when she emerged, her pink glasses askew. "I was just about to close."

"It's late," Brianna agreed. "But I wanted to ask first, do you still have that sticky note pad that Gloria Albright wrote on the other day?"

"Oh, yes," Annalise said in a hushed voice. "That poor woman. Yes, it's under here somewhere. I haven't used it since that day."

Brianna took the offered notepad and stared at the top note. Nothing was written on it, but the indentations of the last message were clear.

"Can I take a few notes off the top?" Brianna asked. "I think it might help the murder investigation."

"What?" Annalise blinked in surprise. "I mean, yes, of course. Whatever you need."

Brianna thanked her, tore off the top few sticky notes, then took her leave. Once inside her own door, she whipped out her phone and pulled up the image of Gloria's lipstick note. As she'd suspected, the spiky handwriting of the suicide note was completely different to the notepad's loopy swirls.

"Gloria didn't kill herself," Brianna whispered.

She shoved the notes and her phone into her pocket, then dropped off her coins and grabbed her trusty baking tin. She'd saved the leftover scones and pastries from the day for her next errand and piled them in the container. Normally she dropped them off at Macy's or Dot's houses, depending on the day, if she had any leftovers at all. She was pretty good at judging the amount of food needed for the café, after months of baking.

Her tin packed, she locked up the café and pushed her bicycle out of the alley where she parked it. The wind had died down, finally. Although the air was chilly, it didn't bite with ruthless vengeance at her exposed skin.

Darkness gathered around Snuggler's Cove like a heavy blanket. This time of the year, with the winter solstice approaching fast, night fell before dinnertime. Brianna switched on her bike lights and watched carefully for traffic. Luckily, few cars whisked by her.

Kettle Lake nestled in a cluster of hills like soup in a bowl. In the darkness, the only hint of the lake lay in a pitch-black expanse inside a ring of lighted houses.

Deciduous trees, barren in the winter chill, lined the gravel lane circumnavigating the body of water. Bushes filled in between their trunks, preventing a view of the lake from this angle. She swerved to avoid a pothole filled with muddy water.

Brianna passed the turnoff to Fireweed Road. She peered at the houses she passed, looking for a log cabin as Hilda had described. Finally, a snug cabin with a warm porch light beckoned, and she turned into the gravel driveway. It wound past a small woodshed to the front door of a single level log cabin with smoke trickling out from a chimney. Beyond it, the placid lake reflected the moon which had just peeked out from a bank of clouds. Conifers covered the shoreline beyond.

Before she could rethink her decision to come here, Brianna knocked firmly on the forest-green door. Footsteps sounded from inside, then the door opened.

"Brianna?" Devon stood in sock feet with a slim-fitting black tee shirt over flannel pajama bottoms. They had the pattern of hockey-playing moose on them.

"I like your pajamas," Brianna said before she could stop herself. "Very patriotic."

"I wasn't expecting visitors," he muttered, his cheeks reddening slightly.

"I have some baking for you." Brianna presented the tin to Devon. "Because you haven't done your scone run in ages. I thought you might be in deficit."

Devon stared at the tin, then glanced at Brianna with a pleased smile. "That was kind. Would you like to come in and help me eat them?"

"Sure, for a minute."

Brianna stepped over the threshold and passed the tin to Devon. He took her coat, and she pulled off her boots and tucked them against the wall.

"Please, make yourself comfortable. I'll just be a minute." Devon waved at the living room area before disappearing into a bedroom on the right. Brianna glimpsed a tartan duvet before the door closed.

She walked gingerly into the main room, which was long, with plenty of windows facing the lake. On the left was a kitchen area with a battered but sturdy-looking oak table and a clean tea towel hanging on the oven door. On the right, a plain green couch nestled against the back wall with a well-loved leather armchair across from it. A wood stove squatted in the corner below a painting of two wood ducks. The décor was comfortable and homey with no pretension, and Brianna settled onto the couch with a sigh of contentment.

Devon reappeared wearing jeans and a sweater. Brianna tried not to smile at his quick change.

"Coffee?" he said. "I just made some."

"Lovely, thanks."

Devon grabbed two mismatched mugs, poured brown liquid from a pot, then walked over and sank onto the other end of the couch. He passed a mug to Brianna, who wrapped her fingers around its warmth.

"How are you holding up?" she asked. "Hilda said you must be going squirrelly here without work."

"It's a lot of time on my own," he admitted. "I ride Sarge a lot. Took out the boat once or twice. Cecelia visits, of course, but she's pretty busy. I'll be glad once this investigation wraps up, or at least my part in it. Shouldn't be long, now."

"Oh?" Brianna raised an eyebrow. "Has additional evidence come to light?"

Devon frowned at her. "You're not still looking into John's death, are you? It's too dangerous."

"I'm in too deep, now. Look what I received in the mail." Brianna rummaged in her purse and withdrew the envelope she'd received that day. Without another word, she pulled out the photos and spread them on the couch cushions between her and Devon.

Devon's face darkened. He picked up the nearest one and examined it—a close-up of Brianna standing beside her bicycle—then he shook his head.

"This isn't good," he said. "You're clearly being warned off the case. Assuming the killer sent these, you now have a target on your back."

"I know." Brianna stared at the photos for a long moment. She shivered. "But it's too late. They know I'm investigating. The only way out of this is if we find the killer."

"Where 'we' is the police." Devon stared at her.

Brianna shrugged. "But if I can help, I will."

Devon scrubbed his face with his hands. "You're infuriatingly persistent," he said through his fingers. "But I'm going to take these photos to the detachment later tonight and get them to monitor you, okay?"

"That would be nice." The amount of relief Devon's words triggered surprised Brianna.

"Good. I'll swing by frequently, too. Can't hurt to be seen with protection. If the killer is watching"—Devon tapped the photos with a long finger—"and they apparently are, they'll take note."

"So, you think they'll clear your name soon?" Brianna looked at him expectantly. "Any reason in particular?"

Devon stared at her, then he chuckled. "You don't give up."

"So I've been told." When Devon didn't immediately speak, Brianna tilted her head. "You had a history with John Albright. It must have been more than a brief acquaintance if you got a leave of absence from the detachment. What's the story?"

Devon played with the handle of his mug without looking at her. Then he sighed.

"It's not something I like to dwell on, that's why I didn't tell you before. John and I were in cadet training together, ten years ago. He was as obnoxious then as he was last week, but I was more tolerant." He shrugged. "Twenty-year-olds just want to fit in, right? Anyway, he and I were in a loose circle of friends at cadet training. But John also fell in with some different types, shadier sorts. We all turned a blind eye until he started turning up with brand new gadgets that I knew he couldn't afford. When I asked his then-girlfriend Gloria, she said she hadn't bought them for him."

"The shady friends?" Brianna guessed.

"The very ones. I followed him after the pub one night. He'd been boasting about his new phone and being cagey about how he'd afforded it.

"I followed him to the back of this dive bar in town. He started getting chummy with two men and a woman. I recognized two of them. One man was a well-known burglar, and the woman was an escort who took rich men away from their homes so her associate could strip the place clean. She called herself the Leopard. They passed John a paper bag with a stack of cash inside. Then he promised them he would sneak into the evidence room and corrupt security footage linking the man to a burglary. John's uncle worked in the department, so he must have thought he could access evidence that way."

"No," Brianna whispered. "And he was training to be a Mountie?"

"Well, exactly. I snuck out of the bar and immediately called the training program with the info. When the word got out, John railed at me for being a rat. Of course, he ratted out his new buddies after that. They weren't too happy about it, I can imagine. His plea bargain was valuable enough that he got out with only a few months, but he was expelled from the training program. Took up journalism instead, and that was the last I saw of him, until last week."

"How were you a suspect in this case?" Brianna

couldn't quite understand the connection.

"It was always possible that John sought revenge after all these years, and I retaliated. It was a stretch but still worthy of investigating. I'll be heading back to work on Friday, though."

"That's good news." Brianna heaved a sigh of relief. She hadn't enjoyed suspecting Devon of murdering John Albright, both because it had seemed a ridiculous notion and because they were friends, but she hadn't wanted to let her prejudices blind her. Thankfully, the detectives on the case had given him their seal of approval.

She glanced out the dark window toward the lake. Something metallic glinted in the porch light. She pointed. "Is that your boat?"

"Sure is." He nodded with a smile. "It's only a dinghy, but it gets me around. I can catch fish in it, and that's all I need." He glanced at her. "We could go fishing sometime."

"I'd love to try." Brianna beamed at him. "That smoked trout you gave me ages ago was divine."

"Good. It's a date." Devon's cheeks colored. "That's not what I meant. I mean, it'll happen soon. Well, not soon, because the fish don't bite much in the winter. It's slow going. But maybe in the spring."

"Come by the café, and we'll arrange it." Brianna deftly ignored Devon's slip-up and pushed herself to her feet. "I'd better get going before Paprika sends out a search party."

Chapter 14

Paprika had not sent out a search party. Instead, the ginger cat luxuriated on the window seat across from the propane fireplace that Brianna had left burning low for her. Brianna laughed when she entered after Devon had given her and her bicycle a ride home. She sat next to her lounging cat for a belly scratch.

After a late dinner, Brianna settled onto the couch with a new-to-her cookbook she'd bought a few days ago at the local secondhand bookshop. She spent almost an hour perusing the pages and was only startled out of her happy food reveries by a knock on the door.

"Macy?" Brianna stared at her friend when she opened the float home door. "What's up? It's very late."

Her friend stood on the dock, her hands fidgeting with her clothes. She bit her lip. "There's something I need to tell you," she whispered. "Can I come in?"

"Of course." Brianna ushered Macy inside and closed the door against the winter chill. She followed her friend to the couch. "Would you like some tea?"

"No, no." Macy patted the couch cushion with distraction. "No, I just ate. I was at Costas's house for dinner." She gulped and gave Brianna a guilty glance. "He invited me."

"That sounds nice," Brianna said in a neutral tone. Personally, she wouldn't spend an evening alone with a potential murderer, but Macy was convinced of his innocence. Brianna hoped she was right.

"It was, until I found something." Macy's mouth twisted with pain, and she paused for a long breath. "Costas left me alone in the living room while he went to check on dinner. I was poking into his old photo albums like a big snooper. I'm a sucker for baby pictures, you know?"

"You do work with kids for a living."

"Right! I'm justified. Anyway, I found an album that looked about the right age—the dates lined up—so I flipped through it. The pictures looked to be from Greece, no surprise there. No baby pictures until I saw the christening announcement." Macy swallowed. "The baby's name was Antonis Michelakis."

Brianna blinked at Macy. She'd read that name only yesterday.

"And who is Antonis Michelakis to Costas?" she breathed.

"There was a picture of little Antonis on the next page. Guess what birthmark was on his face?"

"Are you saying the baby was Costas? Did he change his name?"

"He must have," Macy whispered. "He said he had some family troubles. But he never said how big those troubles were. Big enough to create a whole new identity when he moved to Canada, maybe?"

Brianna stood, her eyes scanning the float home's living room. Her gaze stopped on a sheaf of crumpled papers on the side table, and she swooped them up.

"What is it?" Macy said, her eyes staring at Brianna from her pale face.

"These are papers from John Albright's trash can in the Bumblebee," Brianna said absently. Her fingers flicked through the papers. "Hilda Button's daughter took them out to recycle them properly, and Hilda snatched them like the gossip queen she is. The papers are rough drafts of John's crime family book. Ah ha!"

Brianna strode back to the couch and flopped next to Macy, who crowded next to her. They stared at Brianna's finger pointing at a name.

"What are you saying?" Macy's voice quavered. "Why was John Albright writing about Costas? What does it say?"

"It says that Antonis Michelakis is the fifth son of Spyro Michelakis, who is the head of the Michelakis extended family. Nominally, they're producers of goat milk products, but they're known as one of the most ruthless crime families in Thebes. The police don't dare to touch them, since half the force is in their pocket. And"—Brianna swallowed hard—"their signature, how everyone can tell when they punish someone, is to leave the body laid out in state with pieces of feta cheese on their eyes."

She and Macy stared at each other. Brianna saw the moment Macy's disbelief changed to hopelessness.

"So, it's true," Macy said, a catch in her voice. "Costas killed John Albright."

"We don't know that for a fact," Brianna said. She stared at the papers in her hand, her eyes unseeing. "But it sure doesn't look good."

"I was at his house tonight. By myself." Macy hugged herself and shivered. "I still don't understand. He's such a great guy. How could he possibly do something like that?"

"Maybe it doesn't seem so bad to him because it's how he grew up." Brianna couldn't believe she was trying to justify Costas's actions, but Macy's heartbroken expression pulled the words out of her. "Normalized it, you know."

"That's almost worse, if he doesn't know how bad it is."

Brianna clutched the papers in her lap. "I can't keep this information to myself. You know I have to take it to the detachment."

"I know." Macy leaned back against the couch cushions, looking drained. "This evidence is too damning. And if he's really the killer, he needs to be held accountable. Stop teaching badminton in school, for one thing. Ugh, what if he'd done something to those kids?" Macy put her hand to her heart. "But how could he? I just can't see it, no matter how hard I try."

"It's hard to believe." Brianna put the papers on her side table and pulled Macy close for a hug. "I hate misjudging people like that. It makes me distrust my instincts, which is a terrible state of being."

"Do you think I'll ever find a decent guy who isn't a loser or an ax murderer?" Macy said with half a sob, half a laugh. "Does he exist?"

"I hope so," Brianna said fervently. Her heart broke for Macy's disappointment. "I hope so, somewhere."

Macy left a few minutes later, after dabbing her eyes with a tissue. As soon as she closed the door behind her, Brianna leaped to work. She dressed in clothes that weren't pajama pants with fluffy sheep on them, gave Paprika a quick scratch behind the ears, and hefted her purse to her shoulder. She tucked the papers inside the main pocket.

The information she was sitting on couldn't wait. Who knew where Costas would go next? If Brianna was right, and the kiwi farmer had killed both John and Gloria Albright, someone else might be in danger. The new journalist Yasmin Nouri, maybe, or the photographer Sam Brown. Or someone else entirely. Oaklyn's comment about a deranged killer murdering at random ran through Brianna's mind. She zipped her coat firmly against the cold and her errant thoughts.

Brianna stepped out her front door onto the dock. Immediately, she wondered if she was being watched. Surely, Costas couldn't watch her every second of the day. She strode briskly to her locked bicycle in the marina parking lot, but every shadow drew her eye, and every puff of bitterly icy wind made her jump.

She pedaled hard through the dark night. The wind pushed at her, making her bicycle swerve, but the roads were empty of cars and other obstacles. Once, a pickup truck barreled toward her, and Brianna's already pounding heart thumped even louder.

The truck zoomed past her without stopping, and she breathed out hard in relief. The detachment wasn't far, and she wheeled into the parking lot a few minutes later. All the doors of the municipal hall were closed, but a light over the detachment's door shone brightly in the night.

Brianna heaved the door open and entered the warm office. Constable Lenox looked up from his position at the desk.

"Brianna West?" he said in surprise. "What are you doing here so late?"

"I found evidence for the John Albright murder case," she said breathlessly. "I need to speak to the detectives. It's late, but are they around?"

"Lucky for you, they're working late today." Lenox pushed to his feet with a groan and waved her to follow him down the hall.

Brianna's nerves twisted. The last time she'd spoken with the detectives, they'd been prickly and unwilling to listen to her. To be fair, Detective O'Sullivan had been pleasant, but Detective Evron had acted just as she'd feared.

But they needed to know her information, and it couldn't wait. Brianna squared her shoulders and marched through the door Lenox held open for her.

The scent of chow mein and fried rice hit her nostrils. The remnants of a takeaway dinner littered one half of the conference table. The other half held laptops and sheaves of paper.

"Brianna West," Lenox introduced her. "She was in the other day. She has more information regarding the Albright case."

Detective O'Sullivan looked tired, but she gave Brianna a small smile and waved at an empty chair. "Ms. West, hello. It's awfully late."

"Yes, I'm sorry, but I didn't want to sit on my evidence any longer than I had to."

Brianna sat gingerly on the edge of her seat. Detective Evron glared at his laptop screen and didn't acknowledge her. Maybe that was for the better. Brianna angled her body to face O'Sullivan more fully.

"We appreciate you coming in," O'Sullivan said.

Brianna placed her purse on the table and pulled out the crumpled papers from Hilda. She spread them out with Costas's old name on the top.

"We found these papers in the recycling of the Bumblebee Bed and Breakfast," Brianna said. "From John and Gloria Albright's room. They look like cast-off drafts from John's book he was writing. You know, the one about Greek crime families."

"We know the one." Evron finally spoke, his voice gruff and annoyed.

O'Sullivan narrowed her eyes at him but only said to Brianna, "Go on."

"I didn't realize the full implication of these papers until my friend Macy visited me tonight. She'd been having dinner at Costas Dimitriou's house this evening, and she saw something." At O'Sullivan's incredulous look, Brianna shrugged. "I know he's under suspicion, but she's dating him and was sure of his innocence. Anyway, she was looking at photo albums while Costas was busy cooking, and she found his old christening announcement. Except his name was different back then. Now, he's calling himself Costas Dimitriou. When he was born, his parents named him Antonis Michelakis."

Evron finally looked at her with interest instead of annoyance. O'Sullivan raised an eyebrow in question.

"Look." Brianna pointed at the top paper. "Right there. The fifth son of Spyro, the head of the family Michelakis, is called Antonis. John Albright knew Costas's secret identity, I'm sure of it. Coincidence or connection?" Brianna leaned back in her chair, her palms sweaty. "I'll let you figure that out."

O'Sullivan stared at the name for a long moment. She and Evron exchanged meaningful glances. Brianna's heart pattered. Had she provided useful information for the case? Could they finally put this whole mess behind them?

"Oh, and another thing." Brianna brought out her phone and the sticky notes from Annalise. "I don't know where you are on Gloria Albright's death, but I suspect it wasn't a suicide. The imprint on the sticky notes shows Gloria's handwriting from when she visited Strings and Things, the yarn shop next to the Golden Moon. It doesn't look at all like the handwriting of her so-called suicide note. As well, the note was written in lipstick, but I'm certain it wasn't Gloria's shade. She favored a deeper cherry red. Krystal Rivero owns a tube of that tomato-red shade, and she would have motivation, given who her child's father was, but there could be others with similar lipstick, of course."

Evron snatched the sticky notes from the table, and the two detectives examined them carefully.

"You're saying you can tell the shades of red lipstick apart?" Evron said, skepticism squeezing out of every pore.

"We can corroborate with forensics," O'Sullivan said absently, her eyes still on the sticky notes. "Thank you for coming in, Ms. West. We appreciate your help."

"Wait, isn't Ms. West the one who had those photos taken of her?" Evron frowned, then turned to her. "We'll get Lenox to follow you home. Can't have you being an unprotected target."

Brianna warmed at the unexpected care. Maybe the gruff detective wasn't that bad. Although he could work on his social skills.

"Thanks," she said. "That would be nice."

Back at the detachment's main counter, Lenox snorted at Detective Evron's request.

"I'll throw her bike in the back of the truck, but I'm not tailing a bicycle."

"That would be great," Brianna assured him. It was late, and the prospect of a warm ride home in a pickup was vastly more appealing than a cold, dark pedal session.

Lenox grabbed keys from a rack behind the counter and shrugged into his coat. Brianna followed him out the door.

"Bring your bike over to the truck," he instructed. "The bed is big enough for it."

Brianna wheeled her bicycle to a police pickup parked in the lot across from the detachment. Lenox heaved the bicycle with a grunt and shoved it in the pickup's bed. He slammed the tailgate shut. Brianna hopped into the cab with a shiver of gratitude at being out of the wind.

"Better turn up the heat," Lenox said gruffly. "Winter has a tight grip on us now." He gave her a side-eye as he turned the key in the ignition. "Just like the grip you have on this case. You sure like sticking your nose into police business."

Lenox spoke more factually than with judgement, but Brianna felt compelled to defend herself.

"Everyone needs a little help sometimes," she said. "And I want the killer brought to justice, the same as everyone else. If I can help in my own small way, you'd better bet I will."

Lenox waved her comment away and backed out of the parking spot. The truck's headlights beamed forward through the dark night and were the only source of illumination once they hit the unlit road.

"You just need to be careful that you don't come to a sticky end when some criminal decides it's easier to shut you up than avoid you."

"The photos were alarming," Brianna admitted.

"Exactly." Lenox's voice took on a lecturing tone, like he was advising school children on appropriate Halloween gear. "Until this case is settled, you need to keep your door locked. Avoid traveling alone, especially at night."

"That's a difficult ask, since I live alone."

"Just avoid lonely spots," Lenox amended. "Anywhere someone could corner you with no one to hear you call for help. And stop snooping around for clues. You've done enough. The detectives can take it from here."

"They looked pretty happy at the news I brought today," Brianna said with a glance at Lenox.

Lenox sighed heavily. He turned a corner onto the main drag of Snuggler's Cove.

"Corporal Moore will be back soon," he said in a resigned tone. "He can deal with you then."

Brianna hid a smile. "I'm glad they cleared his name from this whole Albright mess. It looks like the case will go well soon."

"I don't get many details, since I'm just a local constable."

"It's such a strange case, though," Brianna prodded, in case Lenox knew more than he let on. The case might be almost wrapped up, but that didn't mean she wasn't curious about the details. "That ritualistic thing with the body, the cheese, all of it. So odd."

"Oh, that's clear now. It's the signature move of a crime family from Greece. In Thebes, I believe. The family runs a cheese production facility. They buy most of the region's milk and employ hundreds. Half of Thebes has a connection to an employee, including the police department. They have so many deals they can get away with almost anything, and the police turn a blind eye. If other crime families try to take over their territory, wham! Bodies turn up, laid out for burial with cheese on their eyes. They might even use their facility as a money laundering operation, but they're definitely big-time cheese makers. They're the big cheese in the area."

Lenox snorted at his own joke. Brianna smiled politely.

"Costas Dimitriou is from Thebes, isn't he?" she said

innocently.

Lenox nodded in confirmation, then he narrowed his eyes and glanced at her.

"You're a crafty one, aren't you?" he said. "You know I'm not supposed to say anything about suspects in an ongoing investigation." He turned into the marina's parking lot and pulled into a spot with a view of Brianna's float home. "Here you are. Get into your house and lock that door."

Brianna thanked him for the ride and hauled her bicycle out of the pickup. She locked it up and walked down the gangplank. Lenox didn't leave until she unlocked her front door and waved at him, for which she was profoundly grateful. Costas wasn't behind bars yet, and she'd just delivered some damning evidence against him. If he had even an inkling of her actions, she needed to keep her doors closed. Maybe she would keep her cast iron frying pan beside her bed, just in case.

Chapter 15

Brianna's alarm woke her up the next morning in the predawn blackness of December. She felt distinctly unrested after her late night. Paprika meowed at her when she stumbled downstairs to fix her breakfast.

"I know you're hungry," Brianna murmured to her ginger cat. She opened a can of food and tipped it into Paprika's bowl. "Here's breakfast."

Brianna stumbled into the Golden Moon fifteen minutes later. She pulled out a big bowl of bread dough from the fridge to warm before groping over to the coffee machine. It took way too long to warm up, but finally she stood surveying her dark dining room with her fingers wrapped around a steaming mug.

A deep sigh surprised her. It felt right, though. She was in her beautiful café—with more tinsel than she had expected a month ago—and she and Macy might have solved a mystery. A pang traveled through her gut at the thought of friendly Costas, but she hardened her heart. If he'd murdered John and possibly Gloria Albright as well, he wasn't deserving of her sympathy.

Instead, she focused on the safety her community would feel this holiday season when the killer wasn't on the loose. She sniffed her coffee with appreciation. Speaking of which, she had some baking to do for the Gourmand Society's Christmas dinner. She planned to bring cheese-filled phyllo triangles as her contribution to the potluck. Maybe she would even sneak in some spanakopita if she was satisfied with the recipe. She could prepare the treats today and freeze them to bake later.

Brianna worked hard that morning. She left the Golden Moon to return to her float home for a few hours to say hello to Paprika and do some paperwork, but she came back mid-afternoon to prep for the next day's baking.

Teri had left, and Oaklyn was in her position behind the counter. The dining room was nicely busy with afternoon tea drinkers and children eating mascarpone cupcakes. Brianna sidled next to Oaklyn from the kitchen.

"Smooth sailing?" she asked the teenager.

Oaklyn didn't look at her. "Fine," she said shortly. "Everything's fine."

Brianna stared at her young employee. Everything was clearly not fine, but she wasn't sure how to broach the topic. She knew where Oaklyn's cold shoulder was coming from. Oaklyn cared for Costas, and Brianna had thrown him to the wolves. She considered backing away and ignoring Oaklyn's mood, but then she remembered Macy. Her friend would want her to ask further questions. Brianna suppressed a sigh.

"Are you sure?" she asked. "Is anything wrong that I can help with?"

"You've done plenty already," Oaklyn muttered.

"Excuse me?"

"You went to the cops yesterday." Oaklyn crossed her arms in front of her chest. "And now Costas is in for questioning."

"Your mother and I found evidence," she said gently. "Evidence that we couldn't ignore. Maybe he didn't do it, but it would be unethical to hide what we found. The truth will come out in the courts, but we need to give them all the information for that to happen."

"It wasn't him," Oaklyn declared. "I don't care what you found. It was a mistake, a misunderstanding, whatever it was. Even if you found something, someone must have planted it. Someone framed Costas for this."

"Maybe," Brianna said. "And I hope Costas isn't the killer, I really do. But until we know for sure, I need to do everything I can to help the detectives find the truth."

Oaklyn pressed her lips together. With the conversation clearly over, Brianna retreated to the kitchen. Oaklyn would have to come to terms with this dreadful upheaval in her life. Brianna only hoped that the betrayal of trust wouldn't scar the young girl's psyche too badly.

Brianna pulled on her apron and grabbed a mixing bowl to start her phyllo triangles. As she took ingredients out of the refrigerator and measured them into the bowl, her mind churned over Oaklyn's words. "Someone framed Costas for this."

They were the words of an overwrought teenager bitterly disappointed by the way the world worked. Brianna knew this, but still they repeated in her head again and again.

To slow her whirling thoughts, Brianna heaved a sigh and slapped her palms on the counter.

"What if someone did frame Costas?" she whispered to herself. She could run through the notion as a thought experiment. Maybe that would quiet her brain. "Who might have a motive for that? Who else wanted John and Gloria Albright dead?"

John's death was clearly premeditated. That suggested that the killer knew him and likely held a grudge against him. Costas was the obvious contender—if John's prying into his secret past had aggravated him—but was there anyone else?

Brianna had ruled out Krystal Rivero for John's death, with her excellent alibi and motivation for wanting John alive. Devon wasn't a suspect anymore, either, given his history with John. He had no real motivation to kill John. Gloria could have killed John and then herself, but the evidence pointed to Gloria being murdered, not committing suicide.

Maybe she was going about this wrong. What other clues did she have on the murderer? Someone knew the contents of John's book and could replicate the murderous ritual of a Michelakis family hit. That someone would also know enough to connect the dots that Costas was the son of the feta cheese magnate and use that information to frame him.

Brianna sighed. It all felt so unlikely. Costas was an obvious suspect. For Oaklyn's sake, she continued to prod the situation while she slowly stirred pepper and ground mustard into the grated cheese in her bowl.

The killer was adept at photography or at least had a telephoto lens to snap pictures of Brianna from a distance. Costas's hobby was bird photography.

If she assumed Gloria was also murdered, she was forced to consume sleeping pills until she succumbed, or maybe the killer suffocated her with a pillow then left the pills next to her to stage a suicide. Brianna wished she had access to the autopsy report, which would answer that question in a heartbeat.

But why would Costas kill Gloria? Brianna's hand stilled on her spoon. She hadn't considered that before. Gloria would likely own John's work, but she hadn't seemed interested in her husband's passion project. Would she have carried on his work? It seemed highly unlikely.

Who else would have wanted Gloria dead?

Brianna froze. She stared unseeing at the far wall, her heart pounding. Her memory served up an image of a screaming Gloria. As if in slow motion, her mind's eyes panned sideways to the footprints of the object of Gloria's wrath.

They'd been unnaturally smooth treads. Most people wore sturdy footwear this time of the year with treads that could grip mud and wet ground easily. A pair of flip flops flashed through her mind, and she swallowed. She'd seen someone recently who had only worn flip flops, despite the weather.

Gloria had been yelling at a man in flip flops, Sam Brown.

Brianna leaned against the counter to support herself. Sam was a photographer and could have easily taken photos of her. According to Yasmin Nouri, John mistreated Sam terribly, and some bad blood existed between them. Sam would have known about John's passion project in detail, enough to frame Costas perfectly. Gloria would have answered the door to the mild-mannered photographer. From there, it would have been trivial for the larger man to overpower the slender woman and stage a suicide, killing both his colleague and the journalist's wife.

Except Sam hadn't been on the island the night of John's murder. Brianna's breath came in short, sharp bursts. She only had Sam's word on that. What if he'd lied to her?

Brianna ran to her office desk and scrabbled at her purse for her phone. If Sam had been on the island and killed John, he certainly could have killed Gloria. The handwriting of the note and the color of the lipstick made the case for murder solid in her mind but doubt still lingered. She dialed a number with shaking fingers, needing answers.

"May I please speak to Hilda Button?" she said when a cheery voice answered the Bumblebee's phone. "Tell her it's Brianna West, and it's urgent."

"Hello, my dear," Hilda's voice spoke into her ear a tense minute later. "How can I help you?"

"Did Sam Brown leave town the night of John Albright's murder?" Brianna asked in a rush.

"Let me see." Hilda hummed a tuneless ditty while she thought. "No, I'm certain he's been here every night since he arrived. He orders hot chocolate to be brought to his room every evening, that's how I know. Says it's to wash down his sleeping pills. Rosy complains about it, says if he wants to sleep better he shouldn't have caffeinated drinks right before bed."

Brianna's breath caught. Sam Brown lied about being in town. What other reason would he have to lie, except that he was covering up his murderous tendencies? She still didn't have proof that Gloria's death was murder, but Hilda's last comment slotted everything together.

"About Gloria Albright's suicide on Monday, can you recall whether the label on the sleeping pill bottle had her name on it? Were they prescribed to her?"

"Oh, I don't know," she replied after a moment's thought. "I believe they were an over-the-counter brand. No prescription."

Brianna thanked Hilda in a daze, then hung up. She stared at the wall opposite for a long minute. It was possible that Gloria also took sleeping pills, but the evidence was otherwise overwhelming. Sam Brown was the killer. He had to be. It all fit. Everything except the lipstick color, but maybe Sam stole it or dressed up in his spare time, who knew.

But she'd been so sure of Costas's guilt a minute ago that she didn't trust her conclusions. She needed to run her newest theory by someone else.

Macy wasn't an option—she was too close to Costas for an objective opinion and would likely latch onto Sam as the culprit with glee—so Brianna dialed another number with shaking fingers.

"Devon?" she said when he answered. "I need to speak to you." She didn't want to talk about it over the phone. Seeing Devon's expression as she outlined her theory would tell her far more about his opinions than his voice would. "Can I come by?"

"I'm with Sarge at his barn," Devon said. Sarge, his retired Mountie horse, whickered in the background. "It's close to Snuggler's Cove. I'll text you the address."

Brianna hung up and shoved her phone in her pocket as she haphazardly threw ingredients into the fridge. Her phyllo triangles would have to wait. She had a murderer to uncover and an innocent man to absolve.

Her phone pinged with Devon's incoming message. Brianna pulled out her phone and copied the address into her map app. Sure enough, the barn was only a ten-minute bike ride from her café.

"I'm off for now," she said to Oaklyn when she poked her head through the connecting doorframe. "Grab Annalise next door if you need anything."

Oaklyn waved without looking at her. Brianna shrugged and retreated to the side door and her bicycle. Oaklyn might not be speaking to her much yet, but she was a capable employee despite that. The Golden Moon was in excellent hands.

And Costas's freedom might be in hers. Brianna swung her leg over her bicycle seat and pedaled swiftly down the road northward. Once she had Devon's calm support for her theory, she would tell the police everything.

But not until then. Her skin crawled thinking about marching into the detachment with her new theory. Detective Evron already thought she was hardly worth listening to. What would he think if she came up with an entirely different opinion? He would laugh at her and probably never listen to her again. O'Sullivan, too.

And she could hardly blame them. She wasn't confident enough yet in her idea to tell anyone except Devon. What if she'd missed an important detail? No, she needed someone to vet her.

The sign for a cidery flew past her, then a cluster of conifers, and finally a field with horses placidly munching bags of hay. A distinctive barnyard smell permeated the still air. A large brown barn stood beside an outdoor riding ring. Brianna recognized Devon's small green pickup truck that he'd given her a ride home in the other night.

She rolled up next to it and leaned her bicycle against the barn's wall. With swift strides, she entered the open door of the barn.

The scents of hay, manure, and horse were stronger here. Rustling and the occasional thud indicated the unseen presence of horses in stalls on either side of a wide corridor running the length of the barn. An open door revealed a wall hung with halters, lead ropes, and bridles.

Sarge was tied to two ropes that anchored him to each side of the corridor. Devon stood at Sarge's shoulder, brushing his glossy black coat. When he heard Brianna enter, he turned and smiled with an inquisitive look.

"Hi. I'll be done here soon. Want to lend a hand?"

Devon held out another currying brush. Brianna took it and stared at Sarge. The big horse huffed at her and nuzzled her hand.

Brianna laughed. "Sorry, big guy. I didn't think to bring a treat for you. Can I brush you instead?"

Sarge nudged her hand again. When no food was forthcoming, he huffed again and turned away. Brianna took this as an invitation to step closer to his other shoulder. She gingerly ran the brush along the grain of his hair.

"You said you had something to tell me," Devon said from Sarge's other side. He moved to the horse's head and brushed his forelock.

"I do." Brianna pressed a palm to Sarge's warm flank and took a deep breath. "I don't think Costas Dimitriou killed John Albright, and I don't think Gloria Albright's death was a suicide. I think the photographer Sam Brown killed them both."

Devon stared at her, his hands pausing at Sarge's head. His eyes widened with uncertainty. Sarge nudged his chest. He continued to brush but didn't take his eyes off Brianna.

"How did you come to that conclusion?" he asked. "And have you gone to the detectives yet with this?"

"No, I didn't want to say anything until I'd talked to you." Brianna's fingers tightened on the brush. "I only just told them everything I knew about Costas's likely involvement. And now I'm running back, saying that it's probably someone else. How could they take me seriously?"

Devon didn't dispute this conclusion. "Tell me what made you change your mind."

"Macy was at Costas's place for dinner, and she was snooping around his old photo albums."

"Looking for clues about the murder?"

Brianna raised an eyebrow. "No, of course not. Looking for baby photos of him. Naturally."

"Naturally," he murmured with a twinkle in his eye.

"But she found out that the name he was born with wasn't Costas Dimitriou, it was Antonis Michelakis. And that's the same name I found in some recycled papers of

John Albright's that Hilda found in his room."

Devon closed his eyes briefly. "Was she tampering with evidence?"

"No, the detectives felt those papers weren't important. They were only rough scribbles of that book he was writing about Greek crime families. The detectives must have a copy of John's work elsewhere. But it turns out that Antonis Michelakis is a son of the head of that crime family."

Sarge whickered, and Devon stroked his nose absently. "What did you do?"

"Took the papers and my information to the detachment, of course. It was damning, I thought." Brianna swallowed, her stomach in knots for Costas. If he was innocent—and there was a good chance he was—would the truth come out? "But now I think it might be Sam Brown."

"And why do you think that?"

"Sam would know everything about John's book project. According to him and Yasmin Nouri, the new journalist sent to take over for John on his assignment, John commandeered Sam's photography skills most of the time. In fact, Yasmin even hinted that he'd had a tight hold on Sam. Sam had received job offers from other publications but always turned them down, even when they were a better fit and more pay. Sam insisted he respected John, but it rang false to my ears. Plus, how could he not hate Gloria after the reaming out she'd given him at the wake?"

"Okay, but a disgruntled employee doesn't necessarily mean a murderer."

"Yes, but there's more. He's a photographer, so he could have taken those photos of me, no problem. I thought it was Costas because he likes to photograph birds with a telephoto lens, but it could easily have been Sam. He also lied to me about being out of town the night of John's murder. Plus, they found sleeping pills next to Gloria." Brianna leaned into Sarge's side and stared into Devon's unblinking eyes. "Hilda told me that Sam used sleeping pills frequently."

"Gloria was a staunch Catholic," Devon reminded her. "And egotistical. She would be the last person I'd expect to kill herself. She'd be more likely to justify murder than suicide."

"I found a sample of Gloria's handwriting in a neighbor's shop," Brianna said. "It didn't match her suicide note, not at all. I think it was a set-up."

They stared at each other for a long moment.

Chapter 16

"I don't have any proof that Sam killed John or Gloria Albright," Brianna admitted to Devon. "But the detectives need to consider this angle, surely."

"I'll call it in." Devon pulled his phone out of his pocket with a firm motion. "Save you from ruining your reputation at the detachment."

He flashed a quick smile at her as the phone rang. Brianna managed a half-smile back, but her mind was on Sam Brown and his dastardly deeds. Her evidence might be circumstantial, but everything fit so well together. With the resources of law enforcement behind them, surely the detectives could uncover the truth now.

Devon cursed and shoved the phone back into his pocket. "The call dropped. Reception on this island is terribly patchy. Look, I'll drive to the detachment and report your findings. Like you said, it's probably best if I go alone. With any luck, Sam Brown is still on the island, and they can bring him in for questioning."

"He and Yasmin Nouri were supposed to visit Costas Dimitriou's farm this afternoon for an interview and pictures," Brianna remembered out loud. "So, they must still be around."

"Good." Devon unclipped Sarge's ropes and led him into a stall. Once he shut the half-door, he strode down the corridor. "You can stay here if you like. I shouldn't be long."

"Okay." Brianna watched Devon climb into his truck and drive away. The barn felt empty despite being full of animals. She wandered back to Sarge's stall and stroked his nose when he poked it out of the half-door. "Sorry about the treats," she whispered to him.

Brianna had nothing to do at the barn, and she had just decided to return to the Golden Moon when a chilling thought struck her. She gripped the half-door with white knuckles.

What if Sam took this opportunity to plant more "evidence" at Costas's property? If he truly had framed the kiwi farmer, he must be nervous that Costas hadn't been detained yet. Without a solid conviction, the detectives would still look for suspects, which might put Sam under the microscope.

But if stronger evidence came to light condemning Costas, Sam could walk away from his crimes breathing easy.

Was today Sam's chance to plant something at Costas's farm? Brianna pulled out her phone, but it didn't have reception any more than Devon's had done. She couldn't call Devon and warn him.

Brianna would have to ride to Kiwi Ridge Orchard and keep watch for nefarious activity.

Emboldened by her decision, she gave Sarge one last pat on the nose and jogged toward her bicycle outside. She wheeled it past rain-filled potholes in the gravel driveway to find a smooth section to mount it.

A familiar pickup truck roared toward the horse barn on the road out front. Brianna squinted at it. Sure enough, Magnus Pickleton sat behind the wheel, his voluminous beard wagging with the bumps on the road.

Brianna made a snap decision. Abandoning her bicycle on the grass beside the driveway, she sprinted toward the road and waved vigorously at Magnus.

The pickup slowed and crunched to a stop on the shoulder. Tools in the pickup's bed jostled noisily. Magnus unrolled his window and peered at Brianna.

"What are you doing out here?" Magnus said. "Never mind. What are you flagging me down for?"

"I need to get to Kiwi Ridge Orchard as soon as possible," she panted. "Can you give me a ride?"

Magnus narrowed his eyes at her, then jerked his head to the passenger's seat. "Get in. But I expect a full report of what's happening."

Brianna suppressed a grin—Magnus might scoff at Hilda's interest in island happenings, but he was as much of a gossip collector as she was—and threw open the door on the far side of the vehicle. As soon as she touched down on the seat, Magnus roared back onto the road. With a yank, Brianna pulled her door closed. She groped for the seatbelt.

"What's the hurry?" Magnus asked. He dodged a bicycle on the road with a glare toward the hapless rider.

"I don't think Costas Dimitriou killed John and Gloria Albright," Brianna burst out. "But I think the real killer is about to plant more false evidence on his kiwi farm. I need to stop him, or at least document it so the police can get the truth."

Magnus scowled ferociously, glanced at Brianna, frowned again, then pushed his foot down harder on the accelerator. The old truck leaped forward with a protesting growl.

"Do you know who the actual killer is?" he asked after a moment. "Or just where he might be right now?"

"All the evidence suggests that the photographer Sam Brown did it." Brianna held onto the door handle as Magnus took the corner on two wheels. "But it's only circumstantial. I want to catch him red-handed framing Costas. Then the detectives will have a much stronger case."

"No one who kills in cold blood and desecrates a good feta cheese by laying it on a dead body deserves to run free," Magnus agreed. He pulled onto the road leading past Kiwi Ridge Orchard and slowed. "Where should I park?"

"Just up here." Brianna pointed up ahead where a graceful willow rose from the roadside ditch. Magnus pulled over and cut the engine. The late afternoon was almost silent once the noisy truck coughed to a stop. When Brianna opened her door, a sudden breeze whistled through barren treetops and brought a shiver across her shoulders.

"Thanks for the ride," she said to Magnus through the open door, but he wasn't inside the vehicle. Instead, he stumped around the back of the truck and rummaged in the bed. He held up a crowbar with triumph.

"Perfect for defense." At Brianna's incredulous look, he said, "What, you thought I'd let you chase after a murderer by yourself?" His thick eyebrows met. "Not a chance."

"I'm hoping he won't even see me." Brianna tightened her lips at the thought of Magnus on a stealth mission, but she couldn't deny the comfort of having someone else with her. She moved to the pickup bed and examined its contents for weapons. Magnus might have had a point. It couldn't hurt to be prepared for confrontation with a murderer. "Thanks for coming."

Brianna selected a solid-looking hammer for her weapon. It had a nice heft to it, although she couldn't imagine swinging it at someone.

"Why would Sam Brown do this, anyway?" Magnus said as they walked toward Costas's farm. A sheep stared at them through a fence across the road.

"That's what I'm a little stuck on," Brianna admitted. "Maybe he finally snapped after being downtrodden by John for so long, I don't know. Gloria might have emulated her husband. And how he sneaked around, killing people and taking pictures of me while still doing his job? He's been a busy guy, that's for sure."

"There's the farm," Magnus said a minute later. They'd rounded a corner, and kiwi trellises appeared on the slope ahead. The breeze had kicked up a notch, and Brianna could comfortably describe it as a steady wind. "Now what?"

"Try to sneak up to the barn, I guess." Brianna's plan shriveled in the cold light of reality. Costas's farm was too open for stealth. "Use the cover of the kiwi plants."

Magnus eyed the leafless rows of kiwi vines. To his credit, he didn't voice his misgivings.

Brianna climbed the slat fence surrounding Costas's property and jogged across muddy grass to the nearest kiwi plant. Although each individual plant acted as weak cover, rows of them would shield her and Magnus from prying eyes at the house. She hoped.

She bent at the waist and shuffled between rows underneath the low overhang of vines. A moment of sympathy for Costas flitted through her when she imagined his backbreaking work of harvesting the hairy brown fruits.

She aimed for a small shed at the edge of the rows. It would provide better cover while they scoped out the house and who might be at it. A parked car that didn't look like Costas's van appeared in flashes as she ran through the rows.

Brianna reached the side of the shed and pressed against it. Magnus arrived a few seconds later, wheezing. Brianna pulled out her phone and opened a video app, then slipped it back into her pocket. She wanted to be ready to collect evidence when the time came.

Motion caught Brianna's eye. She wasn't quick enough to stop the figure from swinging a heavy shovel against Magnus's legs. Magnus cried out in pain and dropped to the ground, clutching his knee.

Sam Brown stepped closer to Brianna with his shovel raised. She backed away. Magnus writhed on the ground, but she couldn't help him, not with Sam approaching.

"You shouldn't have come here," he said. His normally bland, pleasant face twisted in a scowl. "Didn't you get the pictures I sent you? Wasn't that warning enough?'

He swung the shovel hard toward her midriff. Brianna dropped her hammer when she sprang away. She ran back through the kiwi vines, bent double, cursing her luck. Sam's footsteps pounded after her. She desperately wanted to make sure Magnus was okay, but she couldn't do anything to help him with Sam at her heels. This chase gave Magnus time to recover in peace.

Errant vines slapped at Brianna's cheeks. She bent even lower to avoid them. Sam's heavy breathing was too close. Fingers grasped at her elbow. She darted to the side to scurry away from the photographer.

The move gave her a little room to maneuver, but not a lot. Sam's pounding feet in his ridiculous flip flops thudded on the dirt behind her. Brianna scoured the trellises ahead for something, anything, she could use to best Sam. Finally, her eyes rested on a long pair of rusty pruning loppers.

She snatched them from their position leaning against a support beam and whirled around, the hefty metal blade facing away from her. Sam pulled up short. His breath came in fast bursts.

"Stay back," Brianna shouted. She bent her knees to give her head more room to stay upright, although the height was a challenge. Vines tickled her neck, but she ignored them.

Sam lunged forward, but she swung the loppers at him. They struck his forearm. He pulled it back and grimaced. Somewhere, he'd lost his shovel, which relieved Brianna.

"Why did you kill John and Gloria Albright?" She hopped backward on bent legs to give herself more room and waited for Sam's answer with her loppers in front of her. Wind tore through the kiwi vines and rattled the branches menacingly. Maybe her questions would distract Sam long enough for Magnus to recover and help her out.

"John controlled every aspect of my career." Sam's eyes were wild as he searched for an opening to access Brianna without contacting the loppers. "Ever since I first started out. He was my mentor, and I looked up to him. Then, it was the little things that crept up—downplaying my abilities, giving me in-house opportunities whenever a better job offer came up, belittling me in the guise of teaching—that layered on each other. He trapped me with his mind games. By the end, I was practically his servant."

Sam's voice had risen by his final words. Brianna opened her mouth to speak, but Sam rolled on.

"I didn't see how he manipulated me into believing myself unworthy for anything other than his assignments until someone else said it aloud. Then, it was so obvious." Sam paused his dance to approach Brianna and said indignantly, "Do you know how many amazing job offers he made me turn down? All so I could photograph his articles and follow him around for his stupid book project. There's a word for unpaid labor, you know."

"So, you killed him? Why now?"

"I was drunk," Sam panted, "and someone opened my eyes to my situation. I snapped that night, throttled John from behind with my bare hands. It seemed so obvious at the time. It gave me a way out and a chance for revenge for years of mistreatment. How could I not take it?"

"Is that what you did to Gloria?" Brianna said. "Did she guess what you'd done to her husband?"

"She deserved it!" A wild note edged Sam's words. "She was as horrible as John. I have no regrets!"

Sam's eyes narrowed, and he lunged forward. His hands opened to grasp whatever he could catch on Brianna. She swung her heavy loppers desperately. When he ducked her attempted blow, she darted through the kiwi row and ran.

Costas's house wasn't far. He clearly wasn't home, given the silence from the house despite a battle going on outside, but few islanders locked their doors. Maybe she could barricade herself inside and have time to call Devon.

"Get back here," Sam shouted from too close behind her.

Sam was gaining on her. The house was too far away, even though Brianna had almost reached the end of the kiwi rows. Sam was at her heels. She had to do something drastic.

Brianna spun on the spot and flung her pruning loppers around in a wide arc. With a thud, the blade end contacted the side of Sam's head. Brianna gasped. Sam's eyes rolled until only the whites showed. He collapsed to the ground at her feet.

Had she killed him? Brianna gingerly approached the photographer, but he didn't stir. She held her fingers in front of his mouth. Small puffs of warm air pressed against her hand, and she sighed in relief. Her blow had been in self-defense, but she didn't want to cause anyone's death, no matter the reason.

A slow clap from behind Brianna made her whirl around.

Chapter 17

Someone was in the field next to the kiwi rows. Brianna scurried out until she stood straight beside the final trellis. Without the cover of the vines, the mounting wind buffeted her side. Stings of chilly rain hit her face.

Yasmin Nouri, the replacement journalist, stood a few paces away. Her pretty face was highlighted by a pair of pouty lips colored a brilliant tomato-red. Her hands joined in a final clap before falling to her sides.

"I have to give it to you," she said with a smile. "Your investigative work is top-notch. If you weren't a liability, I would consider recommending you for a job with the magazine I work for. A nose for a story is something that's hard to teach."

"But now I'm a liability?" Cold shivers trickled down Brianna's spine. Yasmin was slight and non-threatening at first blush, but her legs were wide in a grounded stance, and she casually held a hammer in her hand like she knew what to do with it. Brianna had her loppers, but that was it.

"Unfortunately, yes. This was supposed to be a clean hit, but you're too nosy for your own good." Yasmin tilted her head. "Why do you care so much about John Albright, anyway?"

"I don't. Or, rather, I only care about him as someone who was murdered and didn't deserve to be."

"Debatable."

"But I care about Costas, the person you're framing to take the fall."

Yasmin smiled. "Yes, he was so perfect. John couldn't stop blabbing about his stupid book, and when he discovered Costas was the son of old Spyro Michelakis, he could hardly contain himself. Wrangled an assignment out of our editor to do a piece on the islands just to get free rein to spend time here. His real goal was ferreting out Costas."

Brianna's head was reeling. "But why do you care about John Albright? I thought Sam killed him. What's your role in all this?"

"Sam was a useful stooge." Yasmin chuckled and swung the hammer to rest on her shoulder. She appeared unconcerned about the now-pelting rain and tumultuous wind marring her smooth black hair. "He was so bitter, so worked up about John's stranglehold on his life. That was a pile of tinder easy to touch a match to. Then Sam did all my dirty work. With guidance, of course. He needed a firm hand showing him the ropes." She grinned. "Ha. The ropes. Get it?"

Brianna didn't acknowledge Yasmin's dark, twisted humor, and the other woman continued.

"John and I go way back. He was training to be a cop in Regina, and he met with my crowd. We were good to him, in exchange for getting rid of evidence that would put us away. It was a profitable partnership but doomed to fail." Her voice took on an ugly growl. "He ratted us out. Sold us straight to the cops. Most of my crew got caught, but I snuck away. That day, I swore revenge on the thieving turncoat. My old boyfriend is still locked up, you know. I could have had a much different life if John hadn't told them everything."

Brianna bit her lip. It hadn't been John who had ratted them out. Not initially, anyway. It had been Devon. She was intensely grateful that Yasmin didn't know about his involvement.

"You're the Leopard," she said when it hit her.

"My reputation precedes me." Yasmin's mouth turned up in a smug smile. "That life is far behind me. And now that John is dead, I can move on."

"But why kill Gloria?" Brianna shuffled slowly sideways, hoping to dash to safety, but one raised eyebrow from Yasmin and she halted. They were too close to risk that hammer swinging into her.

Yasmin rolled her eyes. "That wasn't in the plan. In fact, that might have been what gave you more ammunition than I anticipated in your investigation. Once I turned on Sam's thirst for vengeance, it was a difficult tap to close. Gloria had always treated him with the same disdain that John had, then she guessed he was the one behind John's death. He called me late at night, panicked, with Gloria gagged and bound in her room. We had to make a clean sweep of it. Pity, because it means that you have to die, too. What a waste of a clever woman."

The conversation had taken a turn for the worse. Brianna's hands grew cold on her tool from the wind and rain, but she kept a firm grip. She tried to shuffle sideways again, but Yasmin hefted the hammer in her hands, at the ready.

"Don't run," she said sweetly. "You won't get far. Die

with dignity.”

“I’m not dying today,” Brianna ground out. She swung at Yasmin with her loppers. Distracted, Yasmin leaped back. Brianna burst from her position like a sprinter and took off toward the house. She had a vague notion of barricading herself inside while she called Devon.

Searing agony exploded on her calf. She dropped to the ground, crying out in pain. The hammer had struck her leg with a heavy blow.

A second later, Yasmin was on her. She pushed Brianna down and grabbed her hair. With one hand, she yanked Brianna’s head back. The other reached for her neck.

Brianna flailed hard enough to dislodge Yasmin from her position on top, where she fell to the side. Brianna kicked her wildly with her good leg. The other leg screamed at her. She gasped from the pain and hauled herself backward.

“Stay back!” Magnus hobbled out of the kiwi vines, supporting himself with a rake acting as a crutch. His face was bloodless under his beard, and he winced with every step, but Brianna had never seen such a ferocious scowl on him before. That was saying something, as Magnus was a professional scowler.

“What are you going to do about it, old man?” Yasmin yelled. She gave Magnus a dismissive look, then pushed to her feet and stepped toward Brianna. Brianna crawled away, dragging her injured leg.

With a roar, Magnus leaped at the journalist. His rake-crutch flew to the side, and he landed on the woman with a heavy flop. Yasmin shrieked and pushed Magnus's weight off her. In the tumult, she bashed her hammer against Magnus's other knee.

He grunted and curled around his wounds. Yasmin glared at Brianna, who had scrambled to her wobbly feet during the brief battle. Magnus wasn't the Leopard's concern, since he knew nothing except her assault tendencies. Brianna was her true target.

Brianna hobbled away, picking up speed with every step. Her leg screamed at her, but she gritted her teeth and ignored it. Her aim was still the house, but she despaired at making it in time.

With a sneer of rage, Yasmin dived to the ground, and her hand wrapped around Brianna's bruised leg. Brianna screamed from the pressure on her injury.

"Give it up," Yasmin screeched. "I've waited too long for this day to have you mess it up. Leave no trail, that was always our motto. And I won't break that with you or the old man."

Yasmin grabbed her discarded hammer and raised it above her head. The other woman's iron-like grasp on her injured leg trapped Brianna. She feebly kicked toward the journalist, but her opponent merely dodged the weak motion.

With a snarl, Yasmin took a deep breath before the downswing. Brianna threw her hands up to protect her head and closed her eyes.

"Stop!" Devon yelled from the direction of the driveway.

Brianna opened her eyes. Devon's gun was trained on Yasmin. His hands were steady and his glare intense. She gazed at Devon, so Brianna kicked with her free leg harder against the entrapping arm. Yasmin released her with a grunt.

Brianna scrambled away. Pounding footsteps on the muddy grass drew closer.

"Stop," Devon called out again. Brianna looked up. His brows drew together in a ferocious frown as he ran toward Yasmin.

She dropped the hammer and pushed to her feet, but Devon was on her. With deft, practiced motions, he grabbed her wrists and clasped handcuffs behind her back. With a breath, he started his arresting spiel, but his gaze raked over Brianna, assessing for damage.

She nodded at him and heaved herself to her feet. Her injured leg wobbled but held.

"Are you okay?" Lenox asked her when he puffed to her side.

She nodded again. "A bruised leg, but I'll live."

"Can you take this one to the cruiser?" Devon asked Lenox when he finished his speech. When Lenox nodded and put a restraining hand on Yasmin's bicep, Devon walked toward Brianna.

"Are you okay?" he echoed Lenox's words, but his expression held far more concern for her wellbeing. He took off his coat and draped it around her sodden shoulders. "That woman was about to pummel you with that hammer."

"You arrived in the nick of time."

"Are you up for giving a statement?" He looked at her leg, where her jeans had torn and puffy skin was turning blue with bruising. "We can go to the hospital first."

"I'm fine." Brianna winced as she put more weight on her leg. "I'll get checked out later. But we need to help Magnus Pickleton. He's beside the kiwis there, injured. Oh, and Sam Brown is lying in there somewhere in the kiwi vines. He's the real killer."

Devon blinked at her, then gave a crisp nod. "Lenox!" he shouted to his partner. "Bring your cuffs. There's another one."

He ducked under the trellis, followed by Lenox. A few moments later, male voices murmured through the barren vines.

Brianna took a deep, shaky breath. She was alive and almost unscathed. The murderers were caught, and Costas would go free. Her heart jolted when she recalled what was in her pocket.

Brianna pulled out her phone and pressed stop on the video recording. A slow smile crept across her face.

Devon and Lenox eventually returned. Lenox propelled a dazed-looking Sam toward the cruiser and Devon helped Magnus hobble unsteadily forward. Brianna waited until Devon settled Magnus on a lawn chair fetched from the house's porch. Then, she held out her phone.

"Do you want to know who killed John and Gloria Albright?" she said to Devon.

He froze and stared at her.

"Yasmin Nouri was very chatty at the end," Brianna said with satisfaction. "But she didn't know I was recording her every word. I have her full confession on my phone."

Devon blinked. "That's invaluable."

"I thought so."

"You've done this murder thing a few times," Magnus put in. "Getting to know the ropes."

Brianna shuddered at his phrasing, but she couldn't deny that experience had been a good teacher. She knew how important solid evidence was.

"I'll be fine here," Magnus said. "I hear the ambulance coming now. It'll likely be Will Brantley. He was always clumsy as a boy. Here's hoping he can manage my leg."

Devon cleared his throat and turned to Brianna. "Are you ready to come to the station for your statement?"

"Absolutely," Brianna said with a grin. "Let's do it."

Brianna called Macy on the way to the detachment. Macy's gasps of horror at the danger Brianna had been in rivaled her shrieks of delight at Costas's innocence.

"I knew it!" she screamed. "I knew it!"

Brianna held the phone a distance away from her ear and exchanged a humorous glance with Devon at the wheel. Oaklyn's voice filtered through the speaker as Macy babbled the news to her daughter.

"Where are you?" Macy demanded when Brianna pressed the phone to her ear again, hoping her friend's voice was at a safe volume once more.

"Heading to the Mountie detachment to give my statement," she said. "I could use a ride home, though. My bicycle is at Devon's horse's barn."

"I'll drop it off after work," Devon promised.

"We'll pick you up," Macy announced. "Do your

thing, and we'll be there shortly. Come on, Oaklyn."

The phone line disconnected, and Brianna slid the device into her pocket with a sigh.

"I shouldn't be happy," she said to Devon. "After all, two people died in this terrible mess, and two more are probably going to jail. It's a horrible situation no matter how you slice it. But I admit to feeling a certain satisfaction that justice will be served."

"Nothing is set in stone until the trial," Devon warned. He softened the words with a smile. "But that confession on your phone is significant evidence."

"Best not drop it in a puddle, then." Brianna tucked the phone farther into her pocket.

At the detachment, she waited in an interrogation room until Detectives O'Sullivan and Evron bustled inside.

"Hello, Ms. West," O'Sullivan said. Evron merely nodded, but his gaze was keen and interested. O'Sullivan continued, "I hear you had an altercation today and that you recorded most of it. Can we hear?"

Brianna pulled out her phone and pressed play. The three of them listened as Yasmin Nouri outlined her and Sam Brown's role in the murders. O'Sullivan didn't react beyond a tightening of her brow, but Evron's mouth twisted in a satisfied smile.

"I'll need that phone for now." Evron held out his hand in an imperial gesture. Brianna gave him the phone with hesitation. He strode out of the room.

"We'll grab a copy of the recording and send it to the mainland to check for authenticity, then you can have it back," O'Sullivan said in response to Brianna's frown.

"A day or two at the most, then you can pick it up here. Let me get a few details about the time and place of the recording."

Mollified, Brianna answered O'Sullivan's questions.

"You're free to go," O'Sullivan said as she stood. "Thank you for your help."

Brianna stood and couldn't help the small groan that escaped her lips.

O'Sullivan glanced at her leg and torn jeans. "Better get that cleaned up. Do you have a way home?"

"I have a ride, thanks."

Out at the front desk, three people hovered. Macy gasped when she saw Brianna and raced forward to throw her arms around her friend.

"You're okay," she screeched. "Everyone's going to be okay. What a great day!"

"Stop making such a fuss," Oaklyn muttered, but she glanced at the man next to her with a smile. Costas beamed at her and the others.

"Thank you for uncovering the truth," he said to Brianna. "I didn't know what was going to happen. And with my family background..." He scowled, the brief expression of anger incongruent with his usual cheerful demeanor.

"You can't help where you come from," Brianna told him firmly. "Only what you do yourself."

"Very true words," Costas agreed. "But what are we standing here for? You will want to get home, I think."

A wave of exhaustion washed over Brianna, so strongly she almost swayed on the spot. "Yes," she said faintly. "I'd like to go home."

Chapter 18

Brianna checked the time on a large analog clock on the community hall's wall. Trestle tables lined the space, which was rapidly filling with members of the community for the Christmas potluck. Some attendees had even brought festive decorations for their tables, and a rainbow of colorful tablecloths festooned the rows. Happy chatter rose from the crowd, and a gaggle of children raced by Brianna. One boy wore a set of felt antlers. Other community members entered the hall, brushing snow off their shoulders.

"He's supposed to be here by now," Brianna hissed to Esme beside her. She glanced out the window, where fat white flakes drifted lazily from the sky. Not much had accumulated on the ground yet, but the wintery night wrapped around the festive hall like a cozy blanket. "How can we have a Christmas party without Santa? It was my one job, and I blew it."

"I hate to say it, but you did ask the most unreliable man on Driftwood Island." Esme took a sip of bright red punch from a cocktail glass she must have brought with her. "Do you have a backup plan?"

"No, I—" Movement in the entryway caught Brianna's attention. When she recognized Bacchus, she leaped forward.

"Brianna, my dear." Bacchus spread his arms wide as if to embrace the entire room. "So good to see you! What a splendid event.”

He hiccupped, then beamed at her with a vacant expression. His partner Maenad beside him rolled her eyes.

“He’s three sheets to the wind,” she murmured to Brianna. “I don’t know if you want him as Santa tonight. He’s more likely to drop whatever child is on his lap by accident than give them a present.”

Maenad led the happy drunk away to find seating. Brianna wrung her hands together and rejoined Esme.

“Now what?” she said, trying and failing not to sound at her wit’s end. “Bacchus is out.”

“Look around for a replacement,” Esme offered. “Plenty of men around. Trust me, I’ve been looking.” She raised her glass with a grin.

Brianna bit her lip and gazed around the crowded room. She didn’t know many people well enough to ask around. She briefly entertained donning the Santa suit herself but discarded the thought immediately. Children might believe in Santa, but they would surely balk at a high-pitched voice and curves, and she had no Mrs. Claus outfit.

“What’s up?” Devon wandered up to her with Cecilia Yang in tow. He looked handsome in a forest green button-up shirt which suited his dark hair. Cecelia’s gold top shimmered in the low light of the hall, and her heels tapped on the wooden floor. “You look worried. I thought this was a party.”

“Bacchus is too drunk to play Santa,” Brianna said in a low voice.

“Are you kidding me?” Cecelia glared toward her

mother's partner. "That's so typical. You know what? Excuse me for a moment."

Cecelia stalked toward Bacchus and Maenad. Devon stayed beside Brianna.

"I don't want to get involved in that," he whispered to Brianna. "Cecelia and her mother can be ferocious together."

Brianna stared at Devon until he noticed her intense gaze. He shifted uncomfortably.

"You're a man," she said slowly.

"Oh, he certainly is," Esme said. "And a prime specimen at that."

Devon's cheeks tinged with pink. Brianna pursed her lips and waved away Esme's comment.

"I meant you could be my savior tonight." Brianna backtracked. "Santa. You could be Santa tonight."

"That's not the look I was envisioning for our handsome young corporal," Esme said with a shake of her head. "Honestly, Brianna. I didn't realize how your tastes ran."

Brianna ignored Esme and focused on Devon, who looked unsure. "Could you dress up and hand out presents to the kids? As a special favor to me?" She bit her lip again. "I'm not sure who else to ask."

Devon stared at her for a long moment. "I'll want first dibs on whatever food you brought tonight," he said at last, but his eyes twinkled.

Brianna clapped her hands, relieved to have a solution. "Yes, absolutely. Whatever you want. Thank you so much. I feel like being responsible for Santa not turning up would give me bad mojo for years. Is there anything worse than crushing the hopes and dreams of children?”

“It’s up there,” Devon said. “When do you want me to don the red suit? Wow, I must be getting older if I’m on Santa duty.”

“The white beard is fake,” Brianna assured him.

“I like a mature man.” Esme rested her hand briefly on Devon’s arm. When he gave her a strained smile, she laughed and wandered away, saying over her shoulder, “Merry Christmas!”

Cecilia stalked back to them, Bacchus’s rolling belly laughter floating after her. Devon winced.

“I’d better get her a drink,” he said to Brianna. “She looks like she needs it. Find me when it’s time for the beard.”

Brianna nodded, and Devon joined his irate girlfriend. Cecelia’s high-pitched jabbering faded into the general hubbub when Devon led her to the drinks counter across the room.

Brianna sighed in relief. Her Santa woes were solved. She had small presents in a sack, waiting for the big moment, and the suit hung in a locked cupboard, far from prying children’s eyes. Now, she could relax and enjoy the evening.

Her eye caught on a set of new arrivals. Macy shook snow off her hair, then giggled and slid her hand through Costas’s offered arm. He beamed like he was the luckiest man in the world, and Brianna’s heart squeezed for him. For Macy. For both of them. Costas was a free man, and Macy was at the beginning of a promising relationship. Who knew what the future would hold? For today, life looked good for the two of them.

Oaklyn looked faintly nauseated at the sight of her mother and badminton coach arm in arm. Brianna grinned at her headgear.

"You wore the Santa hat I gave you," she said when Oaklyn and the others drew closer. "I didn't know if you would."

"I was told it's rude to not wear a present," Oaklyn said, touching the hat self-consciously, although she gave Brianna a lopsided grin. The hat was velvety black instead of bright red, although the trim was stark white. It matched Oaklyn's aesthetic perfectly, while still giving a nod to the season.

"It's hilarious," Macy said. "And so unfestive, but oh well. It suits Oaklyn. The dinner looks great from here, Brianna. I love the decorations."

"That was all Hilda and her team of volunteers." Brianna waved her arm around to indicate the tinsel garlands and balloon clusters. "I organized the guest of honor. He's flying all the way from the North Pole, you know."

Oaklyn rolled her eyes. "You don't have to pretend for me. Honestly, how old do you think I am?"

Macy elbowed her daughter. "It's fun to pretend at any age. I remember when you were tiny, and we went to see Santa on Oak Island. You wore that red velvet dress, and you were so excited." She pressed a hand to her heart and sighed. "My little pumpkin."

Oaklyn didn't deign to acknowledge her mother's words, but she didn't curb them, either. Brianna exchanged a grin with Costas.

"The badminton team won second place in the tournament," Costas said with a proud smile at Oaklyn. "The girls were amazing. They worked hard and it paid off."

"I heard," Brianna said. "What a triumph."

"They had a good coach." Macy gripped Costas's arm and beamed at him. Oaklyn huffed at her mother.

Brianna's aunt Dot rolled up to the group and threw her arms around each of them in turn. Her flowing poncho was a vibrant red and green tartan, and a fake poinsettia rested in her short hair. Huge, glittery earrings in the shape of Christmas ornaments dangled from her earlobes.

"Merry Christmas, everyone," Dot said. "It's so nice to see everyone here. Oh, and that punch is divine. You must try it. I might have had a few glasses already."

She chuckled and pressed the back of her hand to her mouth. Brianna looked around for her hairy companion.

"I thought you'd bring Zola with you," she said. "Not that I'd condone it, of course—too much food here, and what if she pooped—even so, I'm surprised."

"She's having a lovely time in her barn with a fresh bale of alfalfa," Dot said. "As much as I love her, a party is no place for a goat. But I need to give her a treat sometime soon. I was thinking of visiting Oak Island's mini farm. Maybe when the weather gets better, I'll take her there."

"Lilliput Farm?" Oaklyn's eyes brightened with interest. "I used to love that place. It's a tourist farm, but all the animals are miniature versions. The barns are half size too."

"Even the food they serve in the café there is small," Macy pitched in. "Remember the sandwiches made from tiny loaves of bread? And the mini muffins?"

"It's absolutely the sweetest place," Dot agreed. "It's where Zola was born. They had more kids than they could handle that year, so I adopted her. I like to take her back to visit her mother and siblings occasionally."

Oaklyn asked another question about the mini farm, her usual reticence forgotten. Macy, Costas, and Brianna stepped to the side.

"I'm so happy to see you out from suspicion," Brianna said to Costas. "And I wanted to say that I'm sorry I suspected you at one point."

"No hard feelings." Costas raised his hands. "I understand. It looked very bad."

"They set you up." Macy frowned. "Of course it looked bad when you were framed."

"Yes, so there is nothing to forgive." He smiled at Brianna. "Unfortunately, there was a lot of truth in the framing. I am from the Michelakis family in Thebes. My father holds the city in a—what do you say, an iron grip. His methods are"—Costas grimaced—"not what I would choose. That's why I moved to Canada. I didn't want to be part of that any longer. Not that I ever joined him in the worst activities, but still. Living in Greece was still too close. I needed a fresh start."

"What did your father say when you left?" Brianna imagined Costas on the run from a vengeful parent.

"He didn't understand my desire to leave." Costas shrugged, and Macy squeezed his arm. "But he supported me. Gave me his blessing. Mother sent a

Christmas gift last week. I won't be visiting soon, but I don't have a target on my back."

"I'm glad to hear that." Brianna glanced at a fabric shopping bag hanging from Costas's free arm. "Is that your food for the potluck? Why don't I show you where it goes?"

Macy joined Oaklyn, and Costas followed Brianna to a side room where long tables stretched down the center. They were already groaning with platters of food, salads, breads, casseroles, and many other items. Another table on the other side held cookies, cakes, pies, and everything sweet.

"I brought a fruit salad." Costas pulled a covered bowl out of his bag and opened the lid to show Brianna. At least half of the cut fruit inside was green, and Brianna smiled.

"Kiwis, of course. It looks great. Why don't we put it with the desserts?"

Costas nestled his bowl between a plate of Nanaimo bars and a platter of butter tarts, then left to find Macy again. Brianna surveyed the food tables, her stomach grumbling with hunger.

"Where's your contribution?" a gruff voice said from beside her.

Brianna turned toward Magnus, who was accompanied by the rest of the Gourmand Society, and pointed halfway down the table. "I brought phyllo triangles and spanakopita. I don't know if I'm entirely happy with the recipe yet, but it will do for now."

Hilda leaned forward and peered at the pastries. "Such a beautiful golden color. Maybe we should sample them before everyone else gets their greedy paws on them."

"But we haven't drawn table names yet." Quentin looked scandalized. "We'd be out of order."

"I'm eighty-three years old," Hilda said tartly. "I've done my share of waiting, don't you think? Besides which, we organized this shindig."

"It's all about quality control, darling," Esme said to Quentin with a soothing hand on his shoulder. "What if Brianna is serving substandard fare?"

She winked at Brianna, who didn't take offense.

"Don't let me stand in your way," she said. "Besides, I have another container of them in case they're popular."

Without another word, Magnus whipped a pastry from the plate and crunched into it. Flecks of phyllo landed in his beard. The others followed his example, and silence reigned as they all chewed.

Brianna's stomach twisted. What would they say? Was her spanakopita up to snuff? She'd resigned herself to the fact that what she served in the café was acceptable to Driftwood Island, but she still craved validation. She wanted others to feel about her baking the way she'd felt eating that other bakery's spanakopita, that day on the ferry.

"Well." Magnus swallowed and smacked his lips together a few times. "Well."

Brianna stared at him. What did "well" mean? It wasn't like Magnus to withhold his opinion.

"Oh, darling," Esme said. "It's simply divine. I love the spices you've added to it."

"You said you have more somewhere?" Quentin peeked under the tablecloth. "Where? I want first dibs."

"Excellent, my dear." Hilda patted her lips with a dainty hand. "You've outdone yourself as usual."

"Heavy-handed on the feta," Magnus said. "But a cheese connoisseur like myself appreciates a little extra cheese."

Brianna sighed happily. Maybe she hadn't recreated that other bakery's pastry, but she'd made her own version that people loved. What was the joy of being a copycat, when she could create her own stamp on the food world?

Magnus glanced at a wall clock. His brow furrowed. "It's time," he said. "Dinner. Esme, are you going to do the announcements for us?"

"Of course, Magnus." Esme touched her feather-embedded hair and adjusted her long silver earrings. "Happy to."

She sailed out of the food room, and the rest of the Gourmand Society followed her. Brianna headed straight for Dot's waving hand, where she sat at a brightly decorated table covered with a snowman-patterned tablecloth. Macy, Costas, Oaklyn, and Dot's son Connor sat with Dot, and Brianna slid into place. She smiled at the others, and her heart squeezed tightly. This was her family, now, and she wouldn't give it up for the world.

Their table was eventually called up, and Brianna loaded her plate to the edges. They ate and talked throughout the evening. Bacchus's roaring laughter interrupted their speech on more than one occasion. Macy and Costas gave each other many sappy glances until Oaklyn stalked off in disgust to join her friend at a nearby table.

Once everyone had eaten seconds and tucked into the desserts, Brianna slipped to another table and whispered to Devon. He nodded and rose. Brianna led him to the locked closet in the entry hall, let him inside, and quietly closed the door. After she returned to her table, Esme stood again.

"We have a special award to present," she shouted over the hubbub. "I'm sure everyone has seen the splendid window decorations turning all the shops into a festive wonderland. The shops were competing for the best-dressed window, as judged by the tourism office. They've just given me the result." Esme slit open an envelope and read the contents. "And the winner is the Come Again Antique Shop, with their whimsical display of vintage toys and presents. Congratulations!"

The hall erupted in cheers. Brianna clapped hard along with the rest.

"Sorry your shop didn't win," Macy said to her. "I thought it looked great."

"I can't take any credit. The Gourmand Society did it all. But I appreciate their efforts." Brianna sipped her punch, feeling at peace with the world. "I have plans for next year, don't worry. It was nice to have a little Christmas spirit in the place. Even if Oaklyn didn't approve."

Macy snorted but didn't reply because Esme held up her hand.

"I've just received confirmation that our special guest has arrived." She looked specifically at a gaggle of children at a craft table in the corner. "Did somebody say, 'ho ho ho'?"

The children screamed in delight when a large, red-suited figure burst into the hall from the entryway. He made his way to a chair in the corner, artfully decorated with an arch of fir boughs and twinkle lights above it. Parents ushered shy children forward and jostled to get their cameras ready. Santa's eyes twinkled merrily, and if anyone noticed his beard was unnaturally white and curly, well, they kept the observation to themselves.

He sat each child in his lap, chatted to them quietly, listened intently, then handed them a present of chocolate and an orange from his sack. Brianna couldn't stop smiling at the magic moment that she'd pulled out of her hat, made possible by the man in the red suit.

When the last child had visited Santa—with one trying for seconds before his father pulled him back—he stood and walked toward a nearby table. Krystal Rivero sat there with her roommate Darla. She'd stretched her legs out to accommodate her round belly, but she pulled them in like a startled anemone as Santa approached.

"For the kid to come," he said to her, presenting her with a present from his sack. "Merry Christmas."

Krystal smiled tremulously through tomato-red lips and blinked away tears. Santa waved at everyone as he made his way to the entry hall and shouted a "Merry Christmas" before the door thudded behind him.

Brianna rose and slipped past chattering children and people comparing photos. She exited the hall and knocked on the closet door.

"Who is it?" Devon's muffled voice said.

"It's Brianna."

The door opened a crack, and Brianna squeezed inside. It was a tight fit, since the closet was meant more for brooms and a vacuum, not two adults. A single bare bulb hung from the ceiling and dimly illuminated the space. She was suddenly aware of how close Devon was and how much she liked the scent of cinnamon that clung to him.

"You were incredible out there," Brianna whispered, trying to bring her mind to the topic at hand. She didn't want any passing children to get a hint of who had entered the closet. "Thank you so much for saving my bacon. The kids loved you."

"Glad I could save Christmas." Devon pulled off his beard to expose a grin. "I could get used to the adoration. I see why the big guy does it."

Brianna chuckled. "You need a team of elves first. And Sarge doesn't fly, as far as I know."

"His flying lessons have stalled lately." Devon rummaged in his sack and pulled out a wrapped present that Brianna didn't remember putting in there. "By the way, I have something for you. Merry Christmas." He thrust the present at her.

Their fingers touched, and Brianna felt a zing. She clamped down on the sensation. Devon was dating someone else. He wasn't available. And she wasn't interested in a boyfriend.

So she told herself.

"Oh, you didn't have to—" Brianna struggled for words, even as she accepted the gift. They were friendly acquaintances, nothing more. Was she supposed to have got Devon something, too?

"Don't look so worried." Devon laughed. "It's not—just open it, you'll see."

Brianna narrowed her eyes at him, but she ripped open the paper. Dark blue fabric unfolded into a ball cap with the insignia of the Royal Canadian Mounted Police on it.

"We've upgraded to a new style, and this is an old one that I never wore," he explained. "So, no one will accidentally think you're a Mountie. But I thought, since you insist on investigating suspicious events on the island, you deserve to look the part."

Brianna's mouth twitched. She held the cap up, examined it, then placed it on her hair. With a head tilt, she asked, "What do you think? Part of the team?"

Devon smiled. "Works for me."

Acknowledgements

Thanks to my editor Paula Lester and beta readers Gillian Brownlee, Michaela, and Betabeck for their helpful comments on the manuscript.

About the Author

Michelle Ford adores books, cheese, and the West Coast of Canada. Tying these all together in a cozy mystery bundle was a tasty treat she couldn't resist. Visit kingletbooks.com for more in the Cheese Café Cozy Mystery series.

Michelle also writes urban fantasy novels under the name Emma Shelford. Visit emmashelford.com to find out more.

www.ingramcontent.com/pod-product-compliance
Lightning Source LLC
Chambersburg PA
CBHW021332190726

48288CB00003B/1065